"You looked like yo
Calan said.

"Hmph. A *friend.* Wha
away, her sarcasm true

"Someone you can trust."

That brought her gaze back to his. "Meaning you?"

It was half challenge and half flirtation. He found the combination intriguing. He also found her intriguing. Why, he couldn't say just yet, but he wondered if she'd picked up on it, too.

"I wouldn't leave my girlfriend anywhere, no matter where I was with her, or how much I didn't like her," he said.

"No," she said, contemplating him. "I don't suppose you would."

"Have you eaten anything?"

"Are you asking me to have dinner with you?"

"What if I was?"

"I'd have to be honest and tell you I've already eaten."

"Then my only other option is to offer to walk you to your room."

★★★

Dear Reader,

Seducing the Accomplice came about after writing Odelia Frank's story, *Special Ops Affair* (April 2011). You'll recall Calan Friese, the ex-Delta soldier wrongly suspected of murder and arms dealing with a terrorist. He's a man who's endured too much loss and is driven by vengeance. Now he's back as TES's newest operative.

My favorite part of writing this story was the research. I loved reading about Albania with all its exotic and diversified beauty and history. I also had the pleasure of spending time with a woman who spends most of her time sailing with her husband. When I contacted her, she had written a blog about their sail to the Adriatic Sea, which included a stop in Albania. Between my research and her insight, I gained a fantastic view of the country.

I hope you agree this is a stellar addition to the miniseries, and that I've hit my mark and given you a satisfying read.

Happy reading!

Jennie

Seducing the Accomplice

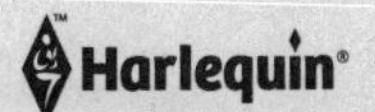

ROMANTIC
SUSPENSE

ISBN-13: 978-0-373-27727-8

SEDUCING THE ACCOMPLICE

This edition published by arrangement with Harlequin Books S.A.

For questions and comments about the quality of this book please contact us at Customer_eCare@Harlequin.ca.

www.Harlequin.com

Printed in U.S.A.

Books by Jennifer Morey

Romantic Suspense

★*The Secret Soldier* #1526
★*Heiress Under Fire* #1578
Blackout at Christmas #1583
"Kiss Me on Christmas"
★*Unmasking the Mercenary* #1606
The Librarian's Secret Scandal #1624
★*Special Ops Affair* #1653
★*Seducing the Accomplice* #1657

★All McQueen's Men

JENNIFER MOREY

Two-time 2009 RITA® Award nominee and a Golden Quill winner for Best First Book for *The Secret Soldier,* Jennifer Morey writes contemporary romance and romantic suspense. Project manager du jour, she works for the space systems segment of a satellite imagery and information company and lives in sunny Denver, Colorado. She can be reached through her website, www.jennifermorey.com, and on Facebook—jmorey2009@gmail.com.

To Barb Sprenger (www.sailbigsky.com)
for helping me visualize Albania and allowing me
to add flavor and detail to this story. She also
taught me a thing or two about navigating a yacht.
My correspondence with her was invaluable,
and she is an acquaintance I will keep.

My agent, Maureen Walters,
for all she's done for me. Keyren Gerlach,
whose edits always bring my stories together.
All my friends and family for their continued support,
and to those who've read and proofed my manuscripts.
Laura Leonard and Julie Dodds, thank you for taking
the time. Special thanks to Susan LeDoux
for all the productive brainstorming sessions.
And Jackie, my twin, I'm glad I have you
along with me for this journey.

And even if I don't say it, as always, to Mom.

Chapter 1

Could a man be too much of a gentleman? Until today, Sadie Mancini wouldn't have thought catering to a woman's needs could be overdone. Her boyfriend had proven her wrong. Somewhere between sailing the Dodecanese islands and arriving in Albania, he'd lost his appeal. He was too conservative, too worried about impressions and impropriety. Fastidious. Fickle. Fake. She'd never thought of herself as a woman who needed a "real man" for a partner, but after spending a sexless week with Adam Khral, she had to reconsider.

Leaving the bathroom stall, she went to the sink to wash her hands. The unfortunate part was that he seemed to really like her. After docking his yacht in Durres, they'd had fun sightseeing all day, and he'd even laughed when she spilled wine on his pants during dinner. The laughter could have been faked, but it was rare that she found a man who accepted her the way she was. She wasn't high maintenance, temperamental or mean—she just hadn't found her niche yet, a place where she fit in. When you were the daughter of a rich man, it wasn't easy finding genuine friends. At least, it wasn't for her.

Why did this constantly happen to her? She *always* realized too late when things were going south. Now she was stuck with Adam in Tirana for the night, and then she'd have to get back on his yacht to cruise home. Timing never worked in her favor. When things fell apart, they fell apart at the worst possible time.

Tidying her sometimes too thick, long black hair, Sadie opened the bathroom door and stepped out into the hotel restaurant, preparing herself for another week with a man she didn't want. She should have spent more time with him back home. Maybe then she could have spared them both.

She could see their table from here and Adam wasn't there. Where did he go? Ignoring a tinge of foreboding, she searched the dining area and didn't see him. Maybe he was in the bathroom. She headed for the table and would have sat, but she saw a wad of euros there. He'd already paid. Unsure of what else to do, she stood by the table and waited, watching the bathroom door. Two men came out, but no Adam. Other diners began to look at her curiously. After ten minutes, she headed for the front of the restaurant. Maybe he was waiting for her there.

But at the entrance, she didn't see him. Was he having issues in the bathroom? She looked back there. No one exited. It had been about twenty minutes since she'd gone to the bathroom. She waited ten more near the entrance, ignoring the glances she received.

Still no sign of him. Had he gone up to their room? But why would he do that without telling her? Why would he leave the restaurant without her? The bad feeling she had expanded into something she couldn't ignore anymore. He obviously wasn't in the restaurant.

Leaving, she rode the elevator to the top floor and walked down the hall to their room. She didn't have a room key so she knocked.

"Adam?"

No response.

She knocked again, harder this time, and yelled, "Adam?"

Down the hall, a man twisted to look behind him. Sadie didn't pay him any attention. Adam didn't come to the door, and she didn't hear the shower running or any other noises.

Trying to calm her anxious pulse, she rode the elevator back down to the lobby and went to the check-in counter where a small, dark-haired woman with big, round brown eyes stood.

"I lost my room key. Can you give me another?" Sadie asked.

"Your name?" the woman asked in heavily accented English.

"Sadie Mancini."

Recognition lit up the woman's face. "A man leave this for you." She handed Sadie a room key with a smile.

Stunned, Sadie took it from her. Why had he left her a room key? He'd left the restaurant without her, he wasn't in the room and now it appeared he'd left the hotel. Had he left without her?

This couldn't be happening. There had to be some explanation. Had there been some kind of emergency?

Not wanting the woman behind the counter to notice how upset she was becoming, she turned and walked back toward the elevators, but once there, she stopped without pressing the Up button. What was the point in going back to the room? She knew he wasn't going to be there. But maybe he left a note.

The elevator doors opened and a man stepped out. Tall with a strong build, he had dark blond hair that looked windblown, as if he'd been outside all day. He nodded a greeting, but she was so disoriented that she didn't think to respond until he'd already passed.

She looked down at the room key in her hand and then back up at the now closing elevator doors. She didn't want to waste time going back up to the room. A note wouldn't change the fact that he was gone and she couldn't wait here and do nothing.

Turning, she caught sight of the blond man heading toward the exit. He was looking back at her. She'd always been transparent. The idea of being stranded in Albania scared her and probably showed. Had the man noticed?

Standing there looking scared wasn't going to help her. Walking briskly toward the front of the hotel, she passed the blond man in the bright and airy lobby and reached the exit.

Outside, there was no sign of Adam.

She still wasn't ready to accept what her gut told her. Rubbing her chilled arms, she looked one way, then the other. It had been nice today but it got cold here in February. She'd definitely need a light jacket tonight.

The blond man spoke with the valet driver, who vanished to retrieve his vehicle. Two cars were parked along the side of the entrance driveway. There were drivers in them. Not seeing another hotel attendant, she waved her hand.

One of the cars drove toward her and stopped.

"How much to take me to the Durres Marina?" she asked through the open passenger window.

"*Parli Italiano?*" the driver queried.

Oh, great. "Do you speak English?"

"Durres." He nodded and said something else in Italian.

She didn't understand him. And he'd likely rob her on the fare because she couldn't negotiate properly with the language barrier. She needed to see if Adam's yacht was still at the marina, but she also needed to save her cash. Just in case.

A man leaned in next to her. She jumped until she realized it was the blond man. She listened to his fluent Italian, not understanding a word but realizing he was negotiating her fare.

The driver nodded. *"Sì, sì."*

Sadie straightened along with the blond man.

"Thirty euros," he said in perfect American English. "He'll take you to the marina in Durres."

"You were listening." He must have come up behind her.

Just then the valet driver appeared with his car.

"You seemed a little lost before," he said to her. "And you're alone. I wanted to make sure you were okay. I'm sorry if I was wrong." His quick glance from her feet to her eyes revealed what might have really motivated his chivalry. But she did like a man with initiative.

"I'm fine, but thank you. As it happens, I needed a translator."

"Will you be all right once you reach the marina?"

"Yes. I'm meeting someone there." She looked down at the room key with a frown before she caught the telling sign. Bringing her head up again, she saw he'd noticed.

"Really, I'm fine." She tried to sound convincing. "Thank you."

Hesitating, he finally said, "Have a safe trip, then," and opened the back door of the taxi for her.

Safe.

She sat inside the car and he closed the door. Straightening, he stepped back. She looked through the window at him until the taxi drove away. Should she have asked him to go with her? Or maybe he'd have given her a ride. Would he have agreed? And would she have wanted him to? She didn't even know him. It would be stupid to risk such a thing. So he'd done something nice—that didn't mean he was trustworthy.

The ride to Durres took forever. She suffered every minute, the entire way wondering if Adam had waited for her. Hoping. But the practical side of her warned her of what she'd find at the marina—or not find.

At the marina, the driver stopped. She stared out the window. What if Adam *had* left her? She glanced down at the room key still in her hand.

The driver said something to her. She caught what sounded like euros and opened her small clutch. Taking out thirty, she hesitated. She took out forty more. Handing him thirty, she held up her forefinger to make him wait and showed him the forty. Then she pointed to the marina.

"Wait?" She pointed at herself, then to the marina, and then back at herself and then down at the backseat. She held up the forty euros and repeated the series of points.

He nodded. *"Sì, sì."* He waved his hand, shooing her.

Getting out, she walked fast toward the docks. She found their dock and made her way to where Adam's yacht should be. But the space was empty. Adam's yacht was gone. Her pulse climbed up her throat. It was dark now, and she could see lights out at sea, but it was impossible to tell which one was his.

He'd left her. And in a smoking hurry. There had been no emergency. And instead of confronting her, he'd abandoned her.

Everything bombarded her at once while she struggled

with the hurt that caused. She was stranded in Albania. Adam had put her passport in his pocket because her clutch was too small. And because he made a point to be such a nauseating gentleman, he'd insisted on paying for everything, so she'd left all her credit cards on the yacht and had brought very little cash. They were only staying one night in Tirana so she hadn't packed much. What was she going to do? Not having a passport was the biggest problem. If not for that, she might have been glad he'd left. How could he have done this to her? When he realized he had her passport, what would he do? Keep sailing?

The jerk!

All his doting had been an act. She wondered what had driven him away. Had she been too strong? Too outspoken? Too klutzy? She hadn't followed his script, so he'd escaped, and if he could dart out of a restaurant as fast as he had to get away from her, he certainly wouldn't turn his yacht around and bring back her passport. He'd probably consider himself lucky that he'd bought himself a few extra days. Less chance of her catching up to him if she couldn't leave Albania for a while.

Coward.

Yes, she wasn't that crazy about him, but he hadn't seemed like the type to abandon a woman in a foreign country. He'd been overly doting, but he'd seemed nice enough. She'd been wrong about men before, but not this wrong.

Heading back toward the taxi, she passed a man who looked at her too long for her comfort. The sooner she got back to the hotel, the better. Although Albania was growing as a country, it was not a safe place for a foreign woman traveling alone.

She should have paid attention to the nagging suspicion that Adam hadn't really wanted to take her to the Mediterranean with him. But she was not one to shy away from conflict, so she'd confronted him.

"Don't you want me to go with you anymore?" she'd asked him after he began talking about canceling their two-week trip.

He'd hesitated. That should have been her first clue.

"Of course I do, sweetie." His sugary reply should have been her second and last. He'd been sticky sweet the entire trip, but it must have been a big fat act. They must have both realized it wasn't working, but, unlike her, he'd bolted as if the restaurant was on fire.

Of course, he'd probably assumed all she had to do was call her father. He didn't know that her relationship with him had deteriorated. She'd never told him that her father was at his wit's end with her. President and founder of a ragingly successful restaurant corporation, her father had always expected her to join the corporate world and take over his empire. She was his only child and a major disappointment. She'd seen it happen to other kids from wealthy parents. Their parents wanted nothing but the best for their kids, for them to succeed the way they had. But when their kids fell short of an insurmountable bar, it was hard to recover from the letdown. It was like settling for less.

Sadie had done well in math and science in high school, but her heart was on canvas. She was more of an artist than a thinker. She loved to paint and had even sold some of her work. The county fair wasn't an art gallery, but hey, she'd sold her work, hadn't she? Why couldn't her dad be proud of her for achieving that? Because he'd be settling for less, that's why. So, Sadie was left in limbo, somewhere between a smart socialite crowd and an ordinary starving artist crowd. She didn't fit in the former, and her father disapproved of the latter. Maybe that was why she constantly embarrassed, annoyed and disappointed those she encountered. She was only being herself, but "herself" didn't seem to fit in.

Her father told her it was because she lacked discipline. She'd been raised in a well-off household with an obedient mother and a driven father. She'd gotten everything she'd ever wanted and more. But her father had never been there and her mother walked through life like a zombie. She wasn't happy. Sadie had always promised herself that she'd never be like that. She'd never marry a man who stomped out her spirit and turned her into nothing more than an enabler to his bloated ego.

Adam was like that. He needed an enabler, and she could not be that for him. But to leave her behind like this? It baffled her that anyone could be so cruel. If she ever saw him again, she'd tear his eyes out. But first she had to get out of this country. And tomorrow wasn't soon enough.

Sitting on the edge of the bed, the phone clammy in her hand from holding it so long, Sadie finally pushed the last number to ring her dad's cell and put the phone to her ear.

"Robert Mancini."

"Dad?" She breathed through her nervousness.

"Sadie? Aren't you on a sailing trip?" With that imbecile boyfriend of hers? She could almost hear him thinking.

"Yes, but…something's happened."

Silence. "Are you all right?" he asked tightly. He knew what was coming.

"Yes. I—I'm fine, I…it's just…well, Adam…he…he sort of…left me in Albania. And my passport is gone."

More silence. "What do you mean 'he left you'?"

"We had dinner and I went to the bathroom, but when I came out, he was gone."

"Did you check the yacht?"

"Yes. I went to the marina and the boat was gone."

"Why did he leave you?"

"It wasn't working out."

"So he just left?"

She said nothing. It wasn't the first time a relationship had ended badly.

He sighed and there was yet another silence. "How many times are we going to go through this?"

Sadie braced herself for his anger.

"I'm constantly bailing you out of these messes. If you'd have gone to college and gotten a real job, none of this would be happening. You'd be a responsible adult."

She was a responsible adult, just not the kind who worked for him. "Daddy, when I first met Adam I thought he was nice."

"You think every man is nice who can put up with you."

She should be accustomed to those types of insults by now, but hearing them from her father always stung.

"I've had enough of your recklessness. It's long past the time you grew up, Sadie Faye. I've been too lenient on you. But now I don't think I have a choice. You're going to have to learn how to take care of yourself."

"I can take care of myself." But he would never see that unless she bowed to his will.

"Then show me. Your so-called friends are always leaving you in the lurch or sticking you with the bill. Your last boyfriend lied to you about his employment status and couldn't pay for any of the trips you went on. You moved in with him and paid for everything, or more like *I* did."

And when said boyfriend grew tired of her, he'd dumped her.

"I could go on for an hour about how many times I've had to pay for your bad choices," her father said.

"But they seem nice when I meet them," she said quietly. She couldn't argue with him in this area. She wasn't any good at picking men with something to offer.

"They know who your father is. They know you come from money. When are you going to learn how to see that? How many times have I had to bring you home after your friends decide to leave without you? This happens to you all the time, Sadie."

"Adam had money. He didn't need yours. That's why I thought he was different." Maybe she was too trusting. She wanted to trust people. She wanted friends she could rely on. Real friends. But above all, she wanted a man who loved her for who she was.

Her father was silent for a long time. "I don't want to do this, Sadie, but I think it's the only way you're going to learn. You're going to have to find your own way home this time. I'm not going to help you. Not at all."

"But..." She was in Albania. Now was not a good time for tough love. He could easily have someone intercept Adam and get her things, her passport most of all. She could be flying home tomorrow.

"Do you have a place to stay?"

"Yes."

"Call the U.S. embassy." He was unbending. "I'll give you the number."

"But—"

"Sadie." His voice was sharp with aggravation.

She didn't protest further. He found her a number and she jotted it down. When he finished, he disconnected.

Numbly, she called the U.S. embassy's after-hours line. Several minutes later, she had made arrangements to go there first thing in the morning.

She checked the time. After ten. There was no way she'd get to sleep any time soon, and she couldn't stay here and climb the walls. The bar had been full when she'd passed it on her way through the lobby. Being around other people, even if she didn't know them or talk to them, would make her feel less alone.

She looked around the empty room. Adam had paid for it. Everything she charged to the room he'd have to pay for. He'd probably known that and hadn't cared. Small price to pay to escape any awkward confrontation with her. But she'd charge all she could anyway. It was her only tangible retaliation until she could get home.

He should feel a lot happier than he did. Calan Friese pulled to a stop in front of the Sheraton Tirana Hotel and got out. Removing a suitcase from the back, he handed the valet parking attendant his keys and headed for the hotel entrance. After six months of ferreting information and tracking down Abu Dharr al-Majid, he'd finally gotten a solid lead. He'd almost caught up to him in Istanbul, where a hotel maid had overheard him on his cell phone telling someone that he was going to Tirana on business. Dharr was in Albania. From there, it hadn't taken long to find him. Calan had bugged his hotel room and waited. After listening to him make plans to meet someone at an abandoned warehouse, he'd decided that was as good of an opportunity he'd have as any. He'd waited in Dharr's car until the meeting was over and surprised him.

Opening the hotel door, Calan hauled the suitcase inside.

It was done. Finished. He'd accomplished what he'd come here to do. The terrorist who'd tried to use a U.S. arms dealer to funnel weapons through an Albanian military export company was dead. Calan had helped to expose the dealer along with a senator who'd bribed the export company to do business with Dharr. Back then, Dharr had escaped. But not this time. Two women Calan loved were dead because of Dharr. After so much time spent hunting him down, it was finally over. Dharr couldn't hurt anyone anymore. Killing him should make him feel good. Satisfied. Triumphant. Instead, he felt…nothing.

He was still never going to see his wife again. He was still never going to see Kate again. Nothing would ease that pain. But justice had been served to a man long overdue for it, a man who needed to be stopped. Calan had stopped him.

Calan pulled the suitcase toward the elevators. The bar was busy tonight. He heard laughter and loud conversation wafting from there. The celebratory sound clashed with his mood. He didn't feel like celebrating, but he should. He was almost angry that he didn't. The world was free of one more terrorist. He could let go of his past now, move on, forget the tragedies and carry only the good memories. But he wasn't sure it would be that simple.

Taking the elevator up and entering his room, he put the suitcase on the king-sized bed. Unzipping it, he lifted it open. Brushing a layer of clothes aside, he found bundles of euros stuffed tight and full inside…to the tune of about three million U.S. dollars.

Calan whistled, a solitary sound in the room. Whatever business Dharr had with the men he'd met at the warehouse, it was worth a lot of money. It also had to be illicit. Anyone doing business with Dharr couldn't possibly be charitable. He'd have to be careful when he left the country. Best not to stay long. Thanks to the company that now employed him, that wouldn't be difficult. He'd be gone before anyone knew what happened.

He closed the suitcase, zipped it back up and put it against the wall beside his bed. Standing in the quiet room, not knowing what he wanted to do now, he sat on a chair near the bed. Leaning his head back, he stared at the ceiling. He was too wound up to sleep. Remembering the noisy bar, he stood again and headed for the door.

It was after midnight on a Thursday and the place was booming. Calan wasn't sure when the busy tourism season started in Albania, or even if there was such a thing, but the hotel had a crowd who felt like drinking tonight. Most of the tall rust-and-black tables surrounding the L-shaped bar were full. Soft light reflected off liquor bottles. He spotted a woman with long dark hair sitting by herself on one of the black bar stools. He recognized her right away. Even from behind she was eye-catching. Not in a model way, in her own special way. She had a presence about her. He'd noticed it when he'd helped her with the taxi. But it was the way she'd looked outside the elevator doors that had initially caught his attention. The doors had opened and there she was, a stunning woman standing with a room key in her hand, looking uncertain and confused and maybe a little frightened. He couldn't have known what was going through her head, but he was sure there had been several thoughts. The racing mind of someone who didn't know what to do. Something had happened to upset her, frighten her, and he'd wondered what that was. Otherwise, she'd have just been another attractive woman he passed in a hotel.

When he'd seen her go toward the exit after contemplating taking the elevator, he'd followed on a hunch. She was alone. There was no ring on her left hand. And she appeared to be American. What was a woman like her doing in Albania? The Sheraton Tirana was a nice hotel, but venture too far from here and things might get dicey in a real hurry.

When she'd gone for a taxi and he'd discovered she was going to the marina in Durres, his concern hadn't waned. He'd heard her trying to talk to the taxi driver. She couldn't speak the languages understood here. He'd helped her get on her way, but he'd wanted to do more. Now she was back at the hotel.

What was her story? Was she in trouble? He intended to find out. Losing two women he loved made him protective of those still living.

He chose the stool to her left. She was drinking wine and her glass was almost empty.

The bartender came over to him. "I'll have a whiskey seven," he said in Italian.

"I'll have another," she said in English, pointing to her glass a few times.

Calan told the bartender to put her tab on his.

The woman turned then. Her eyes were a little red but they were still the amazing blue he remembered when he'd gotten her the taxi. She had a small nose and alabaster skin and full lips with a pronounced heart shape. A good, strong jaw, too. She wasn't beautiful in an all-out feminine way. Her features were stronger than that. No frailty there, which he discovered appealed to him, and that set him on edge. Helping her was one thing, but attraction was something else.

"We meet again," he said, forcing a smile.

When she recovered from her surprise, she smiled back and echoed, "We meet again."

"I thought you were going to Durres."

The smile dimmed until her mouth flatlined and she faced forward to lift her wineglass. She finished off the remainder of wine.

"Change of plans?" he coaxed.

The bartender returned with their drinks. Instead of reaching for hers, she turned to him and observed him curiously.

"Are you a nice guy?" she asked.

It wasn't what he was expecting. "That's one way to put it."

"Every time I meet someone I think is nice, they turn out to be someone completely different." She sounded so sincere.

"I take it the reason you came back from Durres is because someone wasn't nice?"

"That's putting it mildly." She sipped her wine.

"What happened?"

"I sailed here with my boyfriend on his yacht. We were going to spend the night here and then go back to Durres and sail to Montenegro in the morning." She sighed long and heavy, gazing down at her glass. "He's probably in Italy by now."

"He *left* you here?" He cocked his head as he waited for her to answer. Her boyfriend had left her in Albania? Sailed away on his fancy yacht without her?

"Yes."

"Why?" Could there be a good enough reason?

"It wasn't working out and he ran like a coward." She turned those sincere eyes to him. "I know I've annoyed people before, and I've had relationships end badly, but nobody's ever done this to me."

"Never had a boyfriend who'd leave you in Albania, huh?" He had to hide his anger. If the man was here now…

"No." She sipped her wine again.

"What's his name? Maybe I can track him down for you." She didn't have to know he actually could.

"Adam Krahl," she said derisively. "He had my passport in his pocket and I don't have much cash. All my credit cards and clothes are on his yacht. Any decent person would at least make sure I had a passport."

Any decent person would. "The guy is obviously an asshole." Maybe he would track him down after all.

"Yeah. He really didn't care about me at all, did he? I can't believe how easy it was for him to treat me with such heartless disregard. And I didn't even see it coming. Even after I realized we were wrong for each other." Her eyes gave him a slow, tipsy blink. "My father is angry with me for that. He says I need to grow up. That's why he told me to find my own way home." She picked up her wineglass and took another sip. When she set the glass down, it fell over. She picked it up and set it upright on the table, not appearing to care that she'd spilled what remained in the glass. But she looked over at him as if expecting him to comment, the defiance in her eyes warning him that she was ready.

Affection swelled in him. If she was annoying it was because she spoke the truth and wasn't self-conscious about her actions. She was genuine. Clumsy, maybe, but genuine. He took a handful of bar napkins from a holder and sopped up the spilled wine. When he finished, he saw that she was watching him with new interest.

"What's your name?" she asked.

He hesitated. She had nothing to do with his reason for coming here. He didn't see the harm in telling her. He'd be gone in the morning anyway. He just wanted to make sure she was okay. That's all.

"Calan Friese."

"I'm Sadie Mancini." Her S and her C slurred. "I'd say it's nice to meet you but I'm having a hard time thrusting people right now."

He couldn't help grinning. "That's understandable."

"But it was really nice of you to help me with that taxi driver."

"You looked like you could use a friend."

"Hmph. A *friend.* What are those?" She turned away, her sarcasm truer than she probably realized.

"Someone you can trust."

That brought her gaze back to his. "Meaning you?"

It was half challenge and half flirtation. He found the combination intriguing. He also found her intriguing, and because of that, troubling. Kate's image flashed in his mind.

"I wouldn't leave my girlfriend anywhere, no matter where I was with her or how much I didn't like her," he found himself saying.

"No," she said, contemplating him. "I don't suppose you would."

If she only knew. He got lost in thought until she turned her empty glass in slow, clumsy circles and started looking for the bartender.

"Have you eaten anything?" he asked. She was drinking a lot.

"Are you asking me to have dinner with you?"

No, it was just the insane urge to make sure she was okay. He could try to tell himself it was only because she was all alone in a country like Albania, but it was more than that. "What if I was?" he asked anyway.

"I'd have to be honest and tell you I've already eaten."

"Then my only other option is to offer to walk you to your room."

Her eyes had livened since he'd sat down beside her. "Haven't you done enough for me tonight?"

He decided not to respond to that.

"What will you do when you get to my room?" she asked.

"Leave you there and go to mine."

Her eyes blinked warmly. "Why not just stay here and talk for a while?"

Because he was enjoying this far too much.

"It's getting late." He stood and put some cash on the bar. "Come on. Let me walk you to your room."

"You're not one of those overly chivalrous guys, are you?"

"What constitutes overly?"

"Worries too much about appearances. Always does what's right, except 'right' in his mind is warped because he thinks a woman constantly needs to be treated like fragile glass..."

He laughed. "That's your definition of chivalrous?"

"Overly."

"Right. Overly."

He held out his hand. "Come on. I promise to leave you alone until morning." And then he could have bitten his tongue for that last part.

She looked from his hand to the empty wineglass and his untouched drink and then back up at him. "You haven't had any of your drink."

"I don't need a drink anymore." She'd given him plenty of distraction. He was no longer plagued by his anticlimactic reaction to killing Dharr.

She put her hand in his and stood. Then, slipping her hand free, she looped her arm with his and they left the bar.

"This is my biggest problem, you know," she said when they were in the open lobby. "I'm too trusting."

"It's just a walk to your room." He didn't like how good she felt next to him. Pressing the elevator button, the doors opened and he led her inside.

"What floor?"

"The top one."

He pressed the corresponding button. The elevator moved.

She kept glancing at him all the way up. He caught every one but didn't encourage her, keeping his hands at his sides.

The elevator stopped and the doors opened. She stepped out ahead of him.

"Which room?"

She told him and looped her arm with his again. All the way down the hall the energy between them simmered. At her door, she inserted the room key and pushed the door open, turning in the entry to face him. Her blue eyes were alert even with all the alcohol, and her lips had a charmed curve to them. He liked the way it animated her face.

It was definitely time to go. He bowed his head slightly. "Sleep well."

Her animation dimmed and he could tell she was disappointed. "You, too."

Heading for the elevators, he felt her watching him before hearing the door close. Damn, he wanted to turn around and go back. Why? How could he be attracted to another woman so soon? He'd just killed the man who'd taken the last woman he loved. Why should this one have such an impact?

He was making sure she was safe. He'd do that for any woman. After tomorrow, he'd never see her again.

He had a suitcase full of money and someone was going to miss it in a real hurry. He had to leave before the consequences caught up to him.

What would a delay of a few hours matter?

He'd take her to the embassy in the morning, make sure she had money and a passport on the way. Then he'd fly out of here.

He just hoped he wasn't making a huge mistake.

Chapter 2

Bright sunlight filtered through the partially open drapes. Sadie slowly came awake. Rolling onto her back, she blinked her eyes clear.

Where was she?

It all came rushing back. Adam. The bar. That man…

Had she dreamed him?

Sitting up on the bed, she looked around the comfortable and elegant hotel room. He'd come to the bar. Walked her to her room, hinting to the promise of morning. She hadn't dreamed him. He was real. Smiling, she fell back onto the bed, one arm slung over the pillow above her head, charmed all the way to the clear blue sky despite her headache.

Had she really met a living, breathing nice man? No other man had ever gone out of his way for her the way he had last night. He hadn't even tried to get in the room with her. He hadn't taken advantage. He'd just been a friend when she needed one the most.

She sighed and closed her eyes, feeling like floating away on a white, puffy cloud. He was handsome, too. Dark blond hair and blue eyes splintered with gold. Tall and strong.

Rolling her head to the side, she checked the bedside clock. A little past nine. Catching sight of the red light on the phone, she smiled more. She had a message!

Giggling all by herself in the room, she flung the covers off and scooted close to the nightstand, sitting up. There was only one person who knew she was here.

Unless it was Adam. Maybe he'd realized he had her passport.

She picked up the phone and pressed the button for the message.

"Sadie, this is Calan. You met me last night."

The disappointment that it wasn't Adam soon vanished with the sound of Calan's voice. Closing her eyes, she tipped her head back and savored it.

"If you wake before nine, give me a call." He told her his room number. "Otherwise, how about meeting me downstairs for breakfast? I'll be waiting."

Hanging up, she put her hand over her heart. "He's waiting."

Hopping up off the bed, she skipped to the bathroom for a quick shower. A half hour later, she was back in her white halter dress and rushing to the elevators.

Downstairs, she made her way to the only restaurant that served breakfast in the hotel and stepped inside. Searching the tables, she saw him. Her heart beat with a fresh rush of excitement.

He was watching her, sexy and gorgeous. Even all that alcohol hadn't exaggerated that. She was beginning to be glad she got stranded in Albania. Maybe this would turn into a vacation after all.

A hostess asked something in Italian.

“I’m meeting someone. I see him,” Sadie said in English, afraid her swooning was too obvious. She must be glowing like the moon.

Smiling broadly, unable to help it, she approached him.

He stood as she reached the table. She gave him a casual hug before sitting down.

“I’m so glad you left that message,” she said.

“I’m glad you decided to meet me.”

He looked so good in jeans and a white cotton dress shirt with the sleeves rolled halfway up his forearm that she swooned even more, if that were possible. And then she caught herself. What if she was making another mistake, trusting too soon?

A waitress came to take their order.

Calan ordered and then said to her, “Goat cheese omelets. Trust me on this one.”

It sounded good but fattening. She settled back against her chair when the waitress left. “What brings you to Albania? I didn’t get a chance to ask you that last night.”

It him took a few seconds to reply. “I’m a business analyst for Homeland Bank. I came to assess the economic potential of opening a branch here.”

In Albania? Homeland was one of the biggest banks in the United States.

“I travel to a lot of different places.”

That seemed feasible. “Where are you going next?”

“Wherever they want to send me.”

Was he being vague or was it just her imagination? She needed to practice being more cautious. “Where do you live?”

“Just outside of D.C.”

She hadn’t expected her luck to be so generous as to put

him in the same city as her. "I'm from San Diego, but I have an apartment in New York." That was a lot closer…

"What do you do?"

This was where she always felt like hedging. Saying she was a socialite wasn't very appealing, but neither was the truth. "I paint."

"You're an artist?" He seemed impressed. They all were at first.

"Not the kind you're thinking. My work isn't in a gallery anywhere. I sold some prints at a county fair a few years ago." She could see him questioning how she could afford to live in San Diego and have an apartment in New York. He didn't even have to say anything. "My father is founder and president of The Mancini Corporation. Table Mesa Kitchen? Pascoli's? Salt Reef Bar and Grill?" Need she go on?

Calan nodded and she could see he understood. "I've heard of them."

Heard of them but not eaten at any of them? She didn't ask.

"Your dad must be very successful," he said.

"Yes." Very was an understatement.

"Is he wiring you money? You said you didn't have much cash, and you don't have any credit cards."

"No." She braced herself for what came next. "I'll take care of that after breakfast."

She watched him ponder that. "If your father isn't helping you, have you called anyone else?"

"I don't need to. Contrary to what my father thinks, I can take care of myself. It's not the first time this has happened. It's never been quite this bad before, but I've been left holding the bill, as it were. My father thinks I need to learn how to stay away from people who are only using me for money. Or learn how to recognize the bad ones before I find myself in these situations." She turned from his observant gaze and pretended to look around the restaurant, wishing she knew what he was thinking.

She saw their waiter coming with their breakfasts and was glad to occupy herself with something. The aroma coming from her colorful plate made her murmur, "Mmm." She took a bite full of spinach and sundried tomatoes mixed with the goat cheese omelet.

"Mmm," she murmured deeper.

"It's one of my favorites," Calan said with a grin.

"It's one of mine now, too." She ate another bite.

He ate with her for a while, sharing a look with her every once in a while. She fumbled over the temptation to believe he really liked being with her. This was how it always began, with easy camaraderie and the promise of more, only she couldn't remember it ever feeling this good.

He put his fork down, finished with his breakfast. "Would you like me to take you to the embassy? You don't have a car, and you'd have to take a taxi…"

More warmth pooled around her heart. All she could do was look at him and smile her enchantment. He met her eyes and she felt a mutual chemistry simmer to a new level between them. The prowling interest in his blue eyes triggered an answering desire.

"I'd like that very much."

They stared at each other awhile, until Calan's expression changed and he looked away. It was as if something had turned a switch off inside him. Did he regret the offer?

"I don't want to be any trouble," she said, just in case.

Whatever had crossed his mind slid behind a smile. "You aren't. It's just that I have to leave today. I should have left this morning."

Today. He had to leave today. “Oh.” She looked down at her plate.

Reaching over, he put his hand over hers on the table. “But for now, I’m right where I want to be.”

And nothing could have made her happier. “Me, too.”

Calan walked with Sadie out of the embassy. After meeting with a duty officer in the consular section, she had her passport request in progress and was able to arrange a wire transfer of money. As soon as he dropped her off at the hotel, he could leave without worrying about her. Except he still didn’t want to leave. He didn’t understand his difficulty. He’d never felt like this before. He had to put a lid on this, drive her back to the hotel and head for the airport. No more messing around.

Closing the passenger door of the rental for Sadie, he went around the car and got behind the wheel.

“I heard Petrela Castle is spectacular. They serve lunch there,” she said, and her hint didn’t miss its mark.

“I can’t stay,” he said. Not even for lunch.

“Right. You have to go.”

He drove out of the embassy compound. A man sitting in a dark blue Volkswagen Passat caught his attention. He was watching them. Calan pretended not to notice, while apprehension reared up and put him on full alert. Driving out into the street, he watched the rearview mirror.

Sure enough, the Passat pulled out into the street behind him.

A stream of expletives chased through his mind. He’d stayed too long. All because of this crazy attraction he had for Sadie, an attraction he’d half-veiled with concern for her safety. He should have known better. He should have practiced more self-control.

But then, he hadn’t expected anyone to find him this

soon. That revealed a lot about what kind of people the money had come from. Well-connected. Powerful.

No one had followed them to the embassy. He was certain of it. Someone along the way had recognized him. He'd gotten gas. The station was just up the street. Had someone seen him and then watched him turn into the embassy compound? The gas attendant? Someone along the street? It made the most sense. And now the people Dharr had been doing business with not only knew who he was, they knew *where* he was.

Turning onto a one-way street, Calan pressed on the gas. The car followed.

"Where are you going? This isn't the way back to the hotel."

He ignored her. This was going to change her mind about him in a real hurry. Her opinion would erase whatever chemistry that had brewed up between them. He was glad he didn't have time to be disappointed.

Around another corner, he sped past a car, his quick maneuvers making Sadie grab hold of the door handle.

"What are you doing?" She sounded alarmed.

She should be.

Sailing into another turn onto a tree-covered street, he pulled into a parking lot and drove to the opposite side, where pavement gave way to dirt. He drove over that to get to another street.

Sadie screeched, using the dash to keep herself from being yanked around too much.

"Calan? What's going on?" she yelled.

"Someone's tailing us," he said.

"What?" Letting go of the door handle, she twisted around and looked behind them and then pinned him with an intent look. "Why?"

He raced past a stadium, weaving around other cars and

narrowly missing a man who'd started to cross the street. The hotel was just ahead, but instead of going there just yet, he made a left and drove back to the street the embassy was on, turning the opposite direction. When he was sure no one followed, he turned around and drove back toward the stadium, watching for the Passat.

Reaching the hotel parking garage, he parked and shut off the engine. That's when he noticed Sadie staring at him. Her stunning eyes were incredulous and upset.

Here it came.

"Why was someone following you?"

He opened his door. "We have to hurry."

"Aren't you going to answer my question?"

Shutting his door, he started walking around the car.

She stood outside the car and slammed the door shut. "Why do we have to hurry? This isn't my problem, it's yours. Oh, my God, I can't believe this. I've done it again!"

He stopped in front of her, angry that she'd just equated him to her loser boyfriend. "We need to get our things and leave the country as fast as possible."

"What?"

If she had a passport—a legitimate passport—he might be inclined to put her on a commercial flight home. But she didn't. And he refused to risk her waiting here all by herself for days, without him here to make sure she was safe. No way. But she was going to need some convincing.

"You want to go home, don't you?" he asked her.

He started walking for the elevators. Sadie followed, but he was sure that was only because he was going to their rooms. Maybe she thought once she was in hers, she was safe from him. She was safe from him anyway, but she wouldn't see it that way.

In the elevator she folded her arms. "Tell me why someone was following you."

He took in her bright blue eyes. Where once sweet infatuation had glowed, now distrust and anger radiated. Talk about bad timing. Why couldn't he have met her in the States somewhere a year or two down the road?

He moved to stand in front of her. Her brow shot down but she didn't shy away from him.

"I'm still the same man you met last night. Nothing about that has changed. I'm someone you can trust."

"You aren't answering my question. It doesn't make you look very good, you know. It makes you look like a liar involved in criminal activities."

Nothing like getting right to the point. That was what made her so different from other women he met. She was strong and honest but she was also too innocent for his line of work.

He moved closer. "I'm someone you can trust," he repeated.

She grunted, eyeing his advance and stepping back against the wall. "I don't even know you."

"I'll get you home."

"I'll get myself home."

This was hopeless. He cursed himself some more for being so negligent. This mission was different than any other. He'd waited years to see it through. And now this. Resignation sank in and he sighed.

"I really wasn't planning on running into you at the bar. I went there for a drink, that's all." The elevator stopped but he didn't care. Not even when the doors slid open. "I was supposed to be gone early this morning, Sadie. I shouldn't have stayed."

But he had. For her. She blinked with the meaning of that and indecision crossed her eyes.

"Do you want me to apologize for that?" he asked. "I

will, but I won't mean it because I don't regret helping you."

The doors slid closed but the elevator remained still. Silence surrounded them while Sadie continued to waver.

"Who are you, really?" she finally asked.

"Calan Friese. I didn't lie to you about my name, but my passport says something else." And it was one of many.

"Why?"

Telling her now might scare her away. "The elevator stopped."

She looked at the panel.

He turned to open the doors and let her precede him. She walked beside him in silence, withdrawing from him. He sensed it and saw it in her profile. When she opened her room door, he put his hand on it to keep her from closing it in his face.

"It's time to say goodbye," she said emphatically. "I really appreciate all you've done and I really enjoyed meeting you and spending time with you. You have no idea. But you obviously aren't who you said you were. I need to stop involving myself with people like you. My father was right." She tried to force the door shut, but he was much stronger and it was easy for him to keep it open.

Damn, he didn't want to do this. He stepped inside, forcing her to back up and letting the door close.

"What are you doing?" She backed into the middle of the room.

"You weren't listening." He walked toward her. She backed up some more, passing the bed with its lush white comforter until she came against the wall of windows flanked by deep maroon drapes.

Calan put his hands on the window, wide apart and above both sides of her head, leaning closer. Her mouth opened and she looked up at him with big eyes.

"That man saw you with me," he said.

"What man? So what if he saw me with you? I won't be with you anymore as soon as you leave."

"He'll be looking for both of us now."

"How do you know that? He doesn't know me. You're the one he's after."

"He won't catch me."

He watched her fill in the blanks of what he implied.

"But he can catch me, is that what you're saying?"

"Yes, and I can't let that happen."

"What kind of people are after you and what did you do to make them come after you? And you better answer me this time."

He had to tell her something. "My mission involved someone associated with them, and now it's grown into more. I didn't think they were going to find me this soon, but they have. I thought I had more time." More time to spend with her.

"What mission?"

Saying he killed a man wouldn't get him anywhere. "I've told you all I can for now."

Her eyes searched into his, back and forth between the two. "I can't go with you."

Bowing his head, he knew he couldn't leave her here. He hadn't been there for his wife, and years later, his girlfriend. Now both of them were dead. Had he been there, would they still be alive?

Lifting his head, he met Sadie's eyes. He saw them register his turmoil and soften.

"Calan…"

"I need you to come with me, Sadie."

And the reason had been in his eyes only seconds earlier. "I don't have a passport."

"I'll take care of that."

"How?"

He didn't answer. He doubted he needed to. He had ways, and she was beginning to learn that about him. But it was true what he'd said before. He was still the same man she'd met last night. Someone she could trust. He felt her gravitating toward that resolution. She believed him. She believed he was a good man.

As they continued to look at each other, the same spark that had ignited over breakfast returned. Whatever had started between them was too strong, and he'd use it to his advantage if it made her go with him. Better that than find out she'd been tortured and killed after he'd left.

Pushing off the wall, he moved back. "Get your things. We don't have much time."

After another brief hesitation, she assembled what little she had and followed him to the door.

"I must be crazy," she said when they were out in the hall. "I'm glad my dad isn't going to find out about this."

Chapter 3

Calan pressed the End key on his cell phone, finishing a call to the pilot of Tactical Executive Security's plane to let him know they were on their way. He would have called first thing this morning, but after running into Sadie in the bar last night, his plans had changed.

Next, he dialed Odie's secure line. Odelia Frank was TES's lead intel officer, and she'd been instrumental in helping him hunt for Dharr. The counter-terror organization would not be the same without her.

Lifting the duffel over his shoulder, he hauled the suitcase that was still against the wall of his room and headed for the door, lifting his cell to his ear.

Sadie followed. "You lied to me. You told me you were a business analyst."

He glanced over at her as he opened the door. "You're right. I'm not a business analyst, but that's the only thing I lied about." Blunt honesty was the best course with her, he was discovering. When he could be that honest…

The cell rang in his ear.

"I should have known you were too good to be true."

Pulling the suitcase out into the hall, Calan thought it best to ignore her.

"Dad's," Odie finally answered.

Her partner, who was now her fiancé, had opened a bakery in Washington D.C. that doubled as TES's first satellite office. It was a perfect disguise, just like TES's headquarters in Roaring Creek, Colorado—a mountaineering store to anyone outside its walls.

"It's Calan." He checked on Sadie. She walked beside him, listening to his call, no doubt.

"Calan," Odie greeted in a friendly tone. "Did you find him?"

"Yes. It's done. But now I have a different problem."

Odie sighed. "Why am I not surprised?"

Some missions didn't go according to plan and this was one of them. "Someone's tailing me. My target met some people just before I made contact. They didn't see me, but they caught up to me afterward. And quick. Less than a day."

"Hmm…if they can move that fast they must have a sizable network, at least locally. An established organization. Who are they?"

"That's what I'd like to know."

"Where are you now?"

"Albania."

A brief silence passed. "Why haven't you left yet?"

He looked at Sadie and answered cynically, "I was delayed."

Sadie's eyes rolled toward him. Yep, she was listening.

"What delayed you?"

"I'll brief you later. There's more to this that I can't discuss right now. I need a passport. A good one. Can you help me with that?"

"Why do you need another passport?"

He stopped before the elevators and Sadie pressed the Down button. "It isn't for me."

"Who is it for?"

"A woman."

The pause over the phone convinced him that Odie was adding everything up in her head. "Anyone else I'd have to tease, but I know what this mission means to you."

The elevator doors opened. "We need to get out of here fast, Odie." He entered the elevator. Sadie followed.

He could hear Odie tapping away on her keyboard.

"I need a few minutes to work this. Going to have to call you right back."

"Hurry."

"I will." She disconnected and so did he.

"Who was that?" Sadie asked.

"Someone who can help us."

Sadie glowered at him as the elevator doors opened to the lobby. He stepped out with her, rolling the suitcase.

"What about the rental?" she asked when he led her toward the front entrance.

"They know what we were driving. We'll take a taxi."

In front of the hotel, a doorman flagged one over, an unmarked car likely owned by the driver, a local man trying to make a living. Sadie got into the backseat while the driver hefted the suitcase into the trunk and Calan negotiated a fare. She scooted to the far side of the backseat when he got in beside her and propped her elbow on the window frame, pressing her curled fingers against her lips.

Speaking in Italian, Calan told the driver to take them to a restaurant across town. That would buy them some time. They weren't going to get out and go to the restaurant, it would just keep the driver busy for a while. Odie only needed a few minutes.

"You should have left me sitting on that bar stool all by myself," Sadie said.

"I wish I would have."

Dropping her hand, she turned, looking insulted.

"That doesn't mean I could have," he added.

"Why? Because you found me irresistible?" she challenged.

"No. I wanted to make sure you were all right. You were a woman alone in Albania. I couldn't ignore that."

"So if I were a ninety-year-old woman you'd have done the same?"

Was she insulted again? "Yes. And I didn't see any harm in spending the evening with an attractive woman. We were both alone, so why not? How could I have predicted that you would turn out to be something different than I expected?"

After a moment of contemplation, she said, "You turned out to be the same as all the others."

She was wrong, but he didn't see a point in correcting her. He was a lot different than anyone she'd met. He was a lot more dangerous. Too dangerous for her sheltered world. He just hoped she never had to discover that. He also hoped he could get her home before he gave in to the urge to kiss her.

His cell rang.

"Yeah."

Odie gave him an address and Calan told the taxi driver he changed his mind and to take him there. The driver glanced at him in the mirror and nodded.

"Thanks," he said to Odie, careful not to say her name.

"Hurry home."

"Believe me, I will." With that, Calan disconnected.

"Everything all set?"

Without acknowledging her bristly tone, he answered, "Yes. Let's get you home."

Tirana had the look and feel of a big city, but there were signs of a suppressed past. The taxi driver stopped in front of a white, stone-trimmed building with chipping, peeling exterior walls. The first floor was grasshopper green and housed a row of businesses. The upper floors were yellow and an awful salmon color. Clothes hung over dirty windowsills, and a huge sign on the roof advertised beer.

Sadie waited while Calan paid the driver and then slid out of the taxi behind him. The driver opened the trunk and Calan lifted the suitcase out along with his duffel, pulling it toward a sidewalk clogged with pedestrians. They stopped to wait for it to clear.

"Why do you have so much luggage?" she asked. Weird for a man. Men usually didn't pack so much. She wasn't sure how she felt about that. Was he a fashion hound or something?

He just glanced at her without comment.

Hanging her overnight bag over her shoulder, she walked with him along the busy sidewalk. At a shop with the name Kaleshi Boutique printed on a sign overhead, he entered.

Sadie couldn't absorb all the merchandise. There was so much. Pottery, woodcrafts, Albanian flags, T-shirts and more stuffed the small shop from floor to ceiling. There was a layer of dust and it smelled musty, too.

A small man with dark hair and eyes stood behind the counter. Calan said something in Italian she didn't understand. The man looked at Sadie and waved them to follow.

Beyond the counter and in the back of the shop was a

door leading to an office. The man pointed to a chair in front of a screen.

"Sit down," Calan said, putting down his duffel and letting go of the suitcase handle.

Sadie sat, putting her bag on her lap and eyeing the shop owner warily. He took her picture with a digital camera and said something to Calan.

Calan answered. The man wrote down some notes and then disappeared through another door leading even farther back into the bowels of the shop.

"It shouldn't take long. He's one of the best in the region and has the right technology. Up-to-date and cutting edge."

"How comforting. He must service the best criminals. I wonder how many tourists have had their passports stolen because of him."

He went to lean against the wall beside his suitcase, unaffected by her sarcastic, if not accurate, observation. The change in him was astonishing. Her impression of him when he had her giddy with infatuation to this…a shadowy man who obeyed no laws to get what he needed.

"Maybe we should ask him if he has my real passport," she couldn't resist saying.

"I thought you said your boyfriend took it with him when he left you on his yacht."

"He did, but I wouldn't put it past him to hock everything of mine."

"I doubt he would have taken the time."

Although she didn't think he meant it as an insult, he was right. "Yeah, he couldn't get away from me fast enough."

"That's not what I meant."

"Doesn't mean it isn't true."

He made no other comment, nor did he try to make her feel better. What could he say, anyway? Adam wouldn't have taken the time to hock her passport. That was the truth. She wondered if she was headed for the same outcome. Calan had been kind so far, but once she was safe, would he leave her like so many before him? Her gaze traveled over his muscular chest to his narrow hips and lean thighs. What a waste of a perfectly yummy man. Was that the reason she was incapable of pinpointing when a man was bad for her? Maybe Calan's attractiveness blinded her. Last night and this morning, at no time did she remotely suspect he was anything other than who he portrayed. Was that her handicap or was this an exception? Maybe no one would have been able to see the signs in this case. Maybe it wasn't just her and her weakness for trusting people she shouldn't.

A few minutes later, a woman emerged and went to stand at the front counter. Time ticked slowly by.

Periodically, Calan went to the front of the store and checked outside. The shop was silent except when shoppers entered, a steady stream but not overly busy for a Saturday, especially considering how busy the sidewalk was. But, of course, paraphernalia wasn't the owners' main line of business. Most of his wares in the front were dusty and old. Maybe only uninformed tourists wandered in for a look. A look was all she needed to know there was nothing here she wanted.

She didn't even want the fake passport.

The man emerged from the back holding the object of her disdain. He handed it to Calan, who opened it and inspected it carefully. Then he closed it and said something in Italian to the man while he opened his wallet and handed over a wad of cash.

Sadie thought the man thanked him.

She stood up and went to Calan. He handed her the counterfeit passport. She opened it and was amazed at how genuine it looked. There were even stamps on some of the pages.

But something wasn't right.

"This isn't my name."

"Of course it isn't." Lifting his duffel and taking the suitcase handle, he left the back of the shop and headed toward the front.

"Calan…"

He stopped but only so she'd open the front door. When she did, he pulled the suitcase through.

"What if I get caught with this?" She showed him the passport. She'd never done anything illegal in her life.

"You won't. Odie knows what she's doing."

"Who's Odie?"

He glanced at her as he flagged down a driver. "A coworker."

What kind of coworker? "Is she as corrupt as you?"

"Neither of us is corrupt."

"That's debatable. We just left a gift shop that doubles as a counterfeit passport dealer."

He grinned down at her profile and she wanted to know what put that look on his face. Something about her banter appealed to him. Or was it something about her? As she continued to meet his look, infatuation threatened to take over, which made her uneasy because she didn't want to be infatuated anymore. Not with him.

A car stopped in front of them. Calan opened the back door for her. She hesitated. Once she got in, they'd go to an airport and she'd have to use this vile document.

"You don't have to worry," he reassured her. "Nothing bad is going to happen to you. I'm going to get you home."

That damnable attraction, a silly infatuation tickled her soul. She could not keep making these mistakes. With her run of luck, she'd end up stranded somewhere else. But she got into the car anyway.

After negotiating with the taxi driver, Calan leaned against the seat next to her. When she saw that they were going back to the hotel, she asked, "Why are we back here?"

"We need a rental."

"Why didn't we get it before we left?"

He looked at her as if she should know. And that's when it dawned on her. He was being careful. "Oh."

"I didn't want to risk being seen in a rental before we get to the airport."

"Yeah, yeah, I get it."

Sadie went with him to the car rental desk, where they rented a blue Chevy Evanda. From there, they headed out of the city.

For the umpteenth time she questioned her decision in going with him. She didn't want to risk dangerous men doing God only knew to her because she'd been seen with him, but would they have left her alone if she hadn't gone with him? She would have had to wait days for her passport. What if the people chasing him discovered that? Would they assume she knew Calan? His purpose here? Who he worked for? How to find him?

Her gut told her she was better off sticking with Calan. For now, anyway. She just hoped it wasn't her heart wishing for the wrong thing again. Last night had been nice, but upon reflection, there'd been times when he seemed to withdraw. Was it due to his profession? He seemed honest and good but did she want to involve herself with someone like him? No, she could almost hear her father saying. Calan operated outside the law. That made him a bad choice. She had to learn to avoid bad choices. Isn't that the crux of the lesson her father intended for her to learn?

Yes. And she was going to follow through.

Once she was on the plane, it wouldn't be long before she was home. They'd go their separate ways and that would be that. It was better that way.

Calan turned off the highway onto another road. They passed some houses and came to a small airport. A sign at the entrance said *Andoni International Airport.*

"It looks legitimate," she commented aloud. But there had to be something else to this place. It was too strange that he hadn't flown into Tirana, the capital city of Albania, one that had an international airport. A bigger one. A real one.

"Did you fly here because you could do so without anyone knowing?"

She could tell he was surprised she'd thought to ask such a question, which only confirmed she was on the right track. "How much did it cost you?"

"It's just a small, private airport."

He drove into a parking area in front of the main building and found a place to park. Beyond the main building, four planes were parked on the other side of a high fence. In the distance, two helicopters rested near a helipad. Movement caught her eyes. A group of men gathered around the last plane, and they were all armed.

"Is that your plane?"

"Yes." He sounded tense.

Nervous, she first glanced at Calan, then all around them. The airport wasn't a flurry of activity, but there were people outside the building. One car drove toward the exit and a taxi pulled to a stop, where passengers were dropped off. A woman and a man walked across the parking lot. The woman saw the armed men and then her partner did, too. His steps slowed and they conversed back and forth.

"They're looking for me," Calan said.

Sadie turned to the plane again. "Do you think that guard knew who you were? What did he say to you?"

"He said my plane was ready."

"He might have been told to let you through."

"Yeah."

"Word sure got around fast. Someone saw you at the embassy and now this."

He studied her face a while, as if she'd surprised him again.

"We're not flying home today, are we." She wasn't asking.

Calan grimly turned back to the plane. So did she. One of the men approached a man in front of the plane and the two began talking. The man he'd approached waved his hands as if explaining something.

"Is that your pilot?"

"Yes."

"What are they doing?"

"Searching the plane."

And questioning his pilot. Calan didn't say it, but she knew that wasn't a good thing.

The pilot held up his hands as if in protest. Sadie couldn't see his facial features from here, but the way his head and hands moved told her plenty. He was afraid of the man confronting him. Another man emerged from the plane and spoke to the one talking to the pilot.

This was all happening right now, unfolding before her eyes. The pilot was in danger. Those men must know it was Calan's plane. Her pulse quickened. She wanted to leave. Now.

"We should get out of here."

"My pilot…" She heard how torn he felt. His pilot could be in serious trouble and there wasn't anything he could do about it. He was one man against too many. And yet, he couldn't leave the man helpless.

The pilot's interrogator removed a gun from his hip holster. Sadie inhaled and covered her mouth with her hand. The pilot took a few steps backward, holding his hands out as if to ward off the other man.

Calan got out of the car, reaching under his shirt and pulling out a gun.

A gunshot went off in the distance, and Sadie turned in time to see the pilot drop. She screamed. That man was just shot! His unmoving body lay sprawled unnaturally on the ground and his shooter just stood there looking down at him. Was the pilot dead? The horror of it—the suddenness of it—numbed her with shock.

The couple who'd also noticed the commotion ran toward the building as if to seek help. Calan still stood outside the car, gun at his side. He'd been too late.

The men at the plane seemed unconcerned they'd be caught. The very idea of that opened Sadie's mind to the magnitude of danger they were in. Whoever they were up against had nothing to fear. Calan had involved himself in something much bigger than she doubted he'd even realized until now.

Getting back into the car, he backed away from the building and sped toward the entrance. Sadie craned her neck to see the shooter put his gun away and turn to the man who'd emerged from the plane. That one pointed toward the main terminal. The shooter looked there and saw them.

Her whole body trembled with fear. "Get us out of here!"

Calan's face remained set with determination. He raced down the road, flying past the guard shack, who also held a radio to his ear. Dropping that, the guard ran out into the road and aimed a gun at them. Two bullets banged somewhere on the rear of their rental car. Sadie ducked and looked back in time to see the guard go back into the shack. Calan reached the main road and swerved, racing into the turn. The sound of a helicopter gave her nerves a panicked jolt. Oh, God. Peering out the window, she caught a glimpse of it overhead.

"They found us. Oh, my God. They found us."

The helicopter passed overhead and lowered when it was in front of them, turning to face them, scattering three other cars traveling the country road. One slid off to the side of the road and came to a stop. Another drove into the oncoming traffic lane to get past the helicopter, and the third veered out of the way to avoid a collision. Calan drove fast but it wasn't fast enough. The helicopter hovered just above the ground. There were no wires along the sides of the road. Calan skidded the car to a stop, then lifted the gun from his lap.

A gunner in the helicopter fired. Bullets sent pieces of asphalt flying. Sadie didn't think the man meant to hit them. It was a warning. Don't move.

Calan fired and the gunner fell back into the pod of the helicopter. The pilot lifted the bird and Calan began driving again. The helicopter tailed them and then passed overhead, avoiding trees and lowering once again in an attempt to block passage. Calan stuck his gun out the window and fired another silenced shot. The pilot maneuvered the helicopter so that Calan's shot hit metal. The pilot fired at them, hitting the front of the rental, still not trying to shoot them inside the car.

Calan fired a second and third time and struck the front window of the helicopter. The pilot jerked and the helicopter swayed, lifted and lowered before lifting again and flying back toward the airport.

"Is he giving up?"

"They would have put someone on the ground, too." He checked the rearview mirror. "We can't let them catch up to us." Calan put his pistol down on his lap and drove fast toward Tirana.

Sadie watched the helicopter until it vanished from view and then checked the road behind them. No cars appeared.

Facing forward, she gripped the armrest and her breathing eased. Her trembling limbs began to relax.

She eyed Calan's weapon. She hadn't seen him with it before now, but she supposed she wasn't surprised he carried one. "What's going on, Calan?"

"I wish I knew." His grave, intense eyes didn't waver from the road and rearview mirror, but he took out his cell and entered a number.

He had to know something. People wouldn't chase him without a reason. And he'd done something to instigate all of this.

"Why did you really come here?" she demanded.

Passing another car on the road, he ignored her, still wearing that unnerving look. He was worried, and she didn't like that.

Into the cell he said, *"Armend Murati, per favore."* And then after a brief silence, *"Grazie."* He disconnected.

"Who is Armend Murati?" she asked.

"He helped to arrange my flight into Albania."

"Your secret flight that isn't so secret anymore?"

He glanced over at her and nothing more.

She was getting tired of his secrecy. "You need to tell me what the hell is going on."

Chapter 4

"You already know as much as I can tell you," Calan said, turning onto the highway that would take them back to Tirana.

"That you came here on a mission and it had something to do with a *target?*" she challenged. "Does that mean you came here to kill someone?" He'd said he met his target but that was for her benefit. Meeting Dharr wasn't the same as killing him, but calling him a target was enough to reveal his true meaning.

He moved his head to get a look at her, wondering if she was smarter than she appeared. He should have never used that word on the phone with Odie.

"I came here to stop a man from hurting any more innocent people."

"In other words, yes." She stared at him, stunned yet indecisive. "And now his friends are after you."

He didn't respond. She knew too much but not enough to harm TES. He'd leave it at that.

Over in the passenger seat, Sadie was quiet all the way back into the city. Calan drove through downtown and then into another rural area. When he found the poorly maintained dirt road he was looking for, he turned. They passed a run-down building and a moderately sized home in somewhat better condition. Around a few more bends and over several bumps and holes, Murati's much larger, much more maintained residence came into view.

"Wow. Is this where Murati lives?" Sadie asked.

"Yes." He parked along the side of the road.

"What are we doing here? Are we going to talk to him?"

"He isn't home."

"How do you know?" She got out of the car with him. "Oh. The phone call. How could I forget? Where is he?"

"On a business trip."

Murati's secretary had told him he'd gone to Kosovo on business and wouldn't be back for three more days. Convenient. More likely he'd talked to whomever was after Calan and fled in the hopes that the problem would be gone by the time he returned. Meaning, Calan would be dead.

Sadie came around to his side.

He'd ask her to wait in the car but he didn't want her out of his sight. Leaning into the backseat, he dug into his duffel bag for a lead wire and stuffed it into his front pocket.

"Why are we here? Are we going to break in?" she asked.

"This will only take a few minutes. Stay by me and don't say anything."

"I don't want to break into anyone's house."

He began the climb up the slope to the house. Sadie

climbed with him and didn't fight him further. She was too busy navigating the terrain in her shoes.

At the side of the house, he found the phone box and opened it. Two wires went to the main phone line, and two more went to something else. Calan clipped the lead wire to those. Now if there was an alarm system, no call would go out.

Straightening, he caught Sadie's curiously wary look. "Be quiet."

"I wasn't going to say anything," she whispered.

That made him smile. Unpracticed in covert activities, she was tougher than she seemed. He led her to the back of the house and checked for an open window or door. Finding none, he stepped past shrubs and over rock landscaping to reach a bedroom window. The rocks were a little bigger than his fist, so he used one to break the glass. Unlocking the window, he raised it and climbed inside, helping Sadie in after him.

The house was two stories and most of the lower level was a rec room with a wine cellar. Upstairs, Calan took Sadie's hand and led her into Murati's home office, which doubled as a bedroom. Letting go of her, he booted the computer on the huge mahogany desk. No password. He searched Murati's email and file folders. Nothing unusual came up. He kept his computer clean.

He searched the rest of the office and other rooms but found nothing. Frustrated, he led Sadie out of the house through the back door. Now he'd have to wait until Murati returned.

When Sadie saw the Durres marina ahead, hope lifted her spirits. "Are we going to Italy now?" He hadn't said much about where they were going. Even with a fake passport she wouldn't mind getting out of this country, and she knew there were ferries that would take them to Italy.

"No."

Those brief hopes deflated like a beach ball with a hole. "Why are we here, then?"

He parked and got out, taking his duffel bag with him. She followed, watching him open the trunk, unzip the suitcase and reach inside. Sadie moved around the side and caught sight of wads of cash inside the suitcase. A lot of cash. A suitcase full of euros. He took a bundle out and stuffed it into his duffel bag.

Sadie gaped at him. Was it stolen?

He fleetingly met her look and then zipped the suitcase shut.

"Is this why you've been evading my questions?"

Lifting the suitcase out of the trunk, he slammed the trunk shut and started toward the marina with the luggage in tow. Still recovering from her shock, Sadie hurried to catch up to him. Walking briskly, she studied his hard profile.

"How much money is in there?" she asked.

"Stop asking questions."

Like hell she would. "Where are we going? That's a question you shouldn't have any trouble answering."

"You said you wanted to go to Montenegro. We're going to Montenegro."

What? She looked at the row of boats docked along the pier. "We're sailing there?"

"No."

"What are we doing here then? Why won't you tell me?"

They walked to a not-so-bad-looking yacht, where he stopped. Stepping aboard, he turned to offer his hand. She took it, but only because she didn't want to trip in her shoes and fall into the sea.

"Whose yacht is this?" It looked to be close to a hundred feet. Nice. Expensive.

"Ours."

"Do you own it or did you charter it?"

"Chartered it in Orikum."

Still, it had to cost a fortune. "Why? You had the plane in—"

"Contingency," he cut her off.

On deck, she followed him to a sliding door, where he inserted a key into the lock and opened it. Pulling the suitcase with him, he stopped just inside and looked around.

There was a white sofa and chair and a brown leather ottoman next to a dining table with four chairs. He passed that and the galley to reach some stairs that led to the lower deck. He was carrying the suitcase. It had to be heavy with all that money inside, yet he made it seem feather light. Below deck, he found a small cabin with two twin beds and wood paneling. Guest quarters. Opening a closet, he put the suitcase inside and shut it again.

"Let's go."

She followed him up the stairs and outside on the aft deck, where he locked the door and helped her off the boat.

"What if someone finds that money?"

"They won't."

She noticed him look around, constantly vigilant. Anything suspicious he'd have noticed, or more aptly, anyone.

They reached the car and he opened the passenger door for her. She looked longingly toward the marina.

"Get in."

She sent him a sullen look and didn't move. "Why can't we take the boat to Italy and fly home from there?"

"It isn't that simple anymore. Whoever's behind all this knows I flew into Andoni."

In secret.

"I knew I should have taken my chances at the hotel."

"Then I would have stayed with you."

Really? He wouldn't have left her alone? "You mean, if I hadn't have gone with you, you'd have stayed?"

"Of course, I would have. Do you think I would have left the country knowing you had to wait for a passport and couldn't get away if someone came after you?"

That was so sweet. Did she matter that much to him? Or would he have treated anyone the same? Yes. It wasn't she who mattered, it was the principle. He had involved her in his problem and now he felt responsible for her safety.

His fingers under her chin made her realize she'd lowered her head with disappointment. She'd rather he cared for her, not his principles. And that desire was precisely why she'd gone with him. Meeting him had confused her judgment.

"Will you get in now?" he asked in a low, deep voice, wooing her, even though he wasn't trying to.

Fighting off her warming response, she forced her concentration to the matter at hand. "Who knew you flew into Andoni International Airport?"

"Someone with a lot of power."

"Someone like Armend Murati? Is that why you searched his house?" She was not going to stop asking until he gave up and told her what she needed to know.

"Yes."

"Who is he?"

"The Minister of the Interior," he said.

It took her a moment to absorb that. If someone like

Murati was friendly with whomever was after them, they were in far more danger than she could imagine.

"You can't fight them, Calan. Clearly this is way over your head."

"If I don't do something now, it will only follow me wherever I go." He looked at her. "And now you, too."

Yes, and wasn't that just her luck? "What kind of organization bribes a government official like that?"

He cocked his head and lifted his brow.

"Stop telling me not to ask questions." She folded her arms and jutted a foot out.

"I didn't."

"You were thinking it."

He grinned. "Get in, Sadie."

Fighting a responding smile, she averted her attention from his handsome face. "You're impossible." But she got in the car, wondering if she was losing her mind altogether. Was this crazy attraction keeping her at his side?

There was a suitcase stuffed with enough money to get them killed. She had a fake passport and they were going to cross the border to get into Montenegro. Would she be arrested before someone started shooting at them again? She was afraid none of that mattered as long as she was with him.

Much later, Calan turned off the road they'd been following just before reaching Shkoder. It wouldn't be long now before they reached the border. The closer they got, the more nervous Sadie became. Once she was there, she couldn't turn back. She'd have to use her fake passport and cross—hopefully—into Montenegro.

"Are you sure about this?" she asked. "Can't we stay in Albania? Won't that make it easier to find out who's after you?"

"Murati won't be back for a few days. We need a safe place to stay until I can talk to him. You'll be comfortable in Montenegro."

She highly doubted that. Not with him around. As long as she kept having these sparks of attraction, she wouldn't be comfortable. He was too secretive. She could hear her father coaching her on her inability to make wise choices when it came to men. No man she'd ever found had measured up to his standards. Men with money, men without money, even business executives. And every man she'd thought would gain his approval had dumped her. In retrospect, they'd been all wrong for her anyway.

She looked over at Calan. He was much different than any other man she'd met or considered dating. His profession was shadowy. How had he gotten to this point of his life? What had led him down such a dark path?

"Have you ever gone to college?" she asked.

"Yeah. I have a degree in business."

"Business." That explained why he chose "business analyst" for his fake title.

"I was in the Army, too."

"Is that where you got your training to work for a black market bounty-hunting outfit?"

"I'm not a bounty hunter. I joined a cause, that's all. A good one."

"What is the cause?" she dared to ask.

After his lengthy hesitation, during which he glanced at her twice, she could see he'd contemplated telling her. But for whatever reason, he decided not to.

Knowing better than to ask any more about the organization where he worked, she refrained from the topic. Maybe there was another way to get him to reveal something. "What did you do in the Army?"

"I was a major at Fort Bragg. Retired now."

"You retired early." Did his new job have anything to do with that? Had he really retired, or had there been a scandal involved? His secretiveness suggested as much.

"I wanted to move on to other things."

He said it so somberly. Had something happened to make him deviate from the military?

"What things?"

He kept his profile to her, but she could see the subject tore at him.

"Did you retire because you wanted to?" she pressed.

"Yes," he said adamantly. He'd definitely wanted to get away from the Army. Had he been pushed into a corner? Wrongfully blamed? He saw her studying him and said, "Let's just say I lost faith in our military."

That only made her more curious. "Why?"

With a stony set to his mouth, he adjusted his grip on the steering wheel and said no more.

"Are you some kind of anti-government activist?" That would explain his secrecy, but why had he come all the way to Albania?

"No. Nothing like that. Following their rules didn't get me very far, that's all."

Judging by the stiffness of his face, they'd cost him, too. Whatever his reason, it had to be personal.

"Are you married?"

"No."

"Were you ever?"

"Why do you keep choosing the wrong men?" he asked, a deliberate steerage of their conversation. He knew what she was trying to dig up, and clearly her question was off limits, but he may as well have said yes. He'd been married before, and from the looks of it, he'd loved the woman very much and something had happened to jade him, something that had driven him away from the Army. She wanted to ask more questions but held back, sensing it wasn't the time to push.

"Because there is always something wrong with them," she answered. "Look at this situation. I need to stop getting tangled with men like you. I keep making bad decisions."

"I'm not the one who abandoned you."

"No, this is much worse." As soon as she said it, she wished she hadn't. Yes, she was in danger because of him, but he hadn't meant to cause any of this. And this wasn't worse than Adam leaving her in Albania. Strange, how her life could be in danger with Calan and she'd rather be with him than Adam.

Calan caught her looking at him before she realized she was doing that. The tightness above his brow eased and a small smile teased her.

A bump in the road jarred her and a car whizzed past them as Calan drove into a turn. Around the bend, the car had to swerve to miss another approaching from the other direction. That was the third time a driver had done that on their way here. And she thought drivers in the States were bad…

"What's your name?" Calan asked.

"What?" It took her a moment to catch up to him. He meant her fake name. For a moment she was back in that hotel bar. "Oh. Mary Calhoun."

"Good girl."

Just as she was about to ask why, she saw the border station ahead. It was busy with activity. A line of vehicles waited to cross. People walked in front of the customs building.

"Oh, God." She'd never used illegal identification before. What if this didn't work?

He glanced over at her and must have seen her condition.

Her heart hammered and her palms were sweaty and she couldn't breathe.

"It'll be fine. Just don't panic and make them suspicious," he said.

"It wasn't fine at the airport."

"Let me do the talking. Give me the rental papers."

With shaky hands, she removed the documents from the glove box and handed them to him.

Taking them and laying them on his thigh, he pulled behind a line of other vehicles. After a long wait, it was finally their turn. Calan handed their passports and car rental papers to a man in a glass-windowed booth, who studied them for what seemed an excruciatingly long amount of time. Then he peered into the car at Sadie, who held her breath so it wouldn't look like she was breathing like a rabbit.

"Pull over there," he told Calan.

Sadie got dizzy. As soon as Calan pulled away from the booth she let her held breath go and sucked in a deeper one. When Calan drove in front of the customs office and parked, she thought she was going to hyperventilate.

"Calm down," Calan ordered.

"Oh, my God." Sadie couldn't catch her breath. She watched the door to the customs office for someone to come out and descend upon them. So far no one had.

"They're just bored. They aren't going to keep us from crossing. We don't have anything."

"They know we have fake passports." Why else would they tell them to pull over?

"No, they don't."

"What about your gun?"

"It's in a safe place."

Was there such a thing? He probably still had it tucked

in his pants. "They're going to see where the helicopter shot at us."

"One little ding. Stop worrying."

Amazing. He was completely unruffled by this, confident that they'd be on their way in a few minutes. "Why are you so sure?"

"Did you see the way that man looked at you? They just want to have some fun looking."

"What?"

"Look at your legs in that dress. How often do you think they see that around here?"

She glanced down at her knees exposed below the hemline of her dress. Really? That couldn't be it. She looked around the rocky landscape beyond the customs building and then at the busy activity of the border station. The cars not parked near them waited to cross among cyclists with bags of groceries or other items packed in baskets or hanging from their handle bars.

An officer approached their vehicle.

Oh, God. Oh, God. Oh, God.

"Stay calm," Calan said.

As if…

"Open the back," the man said in barely discernible English, leaning low to peer into the car at Sadie.

Oh, God. She saw his gun in a hip holster and swallowed.

Calan got out of the car and went to the back, opening it. Sadie twisted in her seat. She could barely see Calan and the officer. The uniformed man searched the now-empty trunk and then Calan closed it.

The officer peered into the car again and saw the duffel on the back seat. He opened the door and eyed Sadie. His gaze went from her face down to what he could see of her legs past the two front seats. She wondered if he'd be able to see her erratic pulse. He returned his attention to the duffel bag.

Unzipping the bag, the man looked inside. He didn't dig into it, just peered inside and then zipped it shut again. Closing the door, he said, "Wait here," to Calan.

Calan got back into the car and waited with her. A few minutes later, the officer returned with their papers and handed them to Calan through the open window, once again ogling Sadie's legs.

"You free to go," the officer said to Calan and then grinned at her.

While Sadie felt like gagging, Calan thanked the man and backed away from the building, turned and drove down the road into Montenegro.

"That was gross," she said.

Calan laughed. "Thanks for the diversion."

Fingering the soft cloth of a purple T-shirt on a crowded table, Sadie looked over the rest of the Afrodita Boutique's wares. There was so much in the small space that it was hard to register everything. They'd gone to two other shops in Budva, Montenegro, and Calan held the bags from those. He stood behind her, watching as he had at the other shops.

She plucked the shirt from a heaping pile and slung it over her arm. Next, she found a white skirt that would look good with that. Checking the size, she rummaged through the rack until she found one that would fit her. Slinging that over the T-shirt, she found some sandals and a pair of shorts. She didn't need much to get her by. Shoes, underwear, a few clothing items and minimal accessories.

Calan took the clothes and sandals from her when she handed them over. At first she'd worried he'd use the money he'd stolen to buy her some things to get her by, but instead, he'd used a credit card. The name on the card, she was sure, wasn't his, but it showed a modicum of integrity that he hadn't used dirty money.

"You don't like shopping, do you?"

Startled, she looked over at him. "Why do you say that?"

"We started this adventure a little over an hour ago and you're almost finished."

"Not almost. We are finished. I don't need anything else." She was tired and ready to find a place to sleep.

He took the items to the small counter near the back and gave them to the older man with a barrel chest and bushy white eyebrows.

"I would have expected something else," Calan said.

The boutique owner's eyes followed their conversation as he rang up the purchase.

Sadie angled her head as she contemplated Calan. "Why? Just because my father is rich?" The truth was, tired or not, she never spent much time shopping. It warmed her that he'd noticed. He made her feel normal, unlike so many she'd been with before.

"I wouldn't put it so crassly, but yes. Why wouldn't you like shopping if you have the money for it?"

"I do like shopping."

"In a tornado sort of way."

She laughed a little at that. "I don't make a fuss. I know what I like and what I don't."

"You haven't even tried anything on. How do you know everything's going to fit?"

"I can just tell." She'd done a lot of shopping. She knew by the look and size of the clothes if they'd fit or not.

"I have nice sweater for these," the shop owner smiled along with his heavily-accented English. "For cool nights…?" His eyes coaxed as they looked from her purchases to her.

"This is enough, but thanks." Sadie smiled.

"You are from the United States, no?" the boutique owner asked.

"Yes," Sadie smiled again at the nice man.

"What brings you to Montenegro? Honeymoon?"

Sadie's jaw froze open and for a stunned moment she didn't know what to say. "Ah…no."

"You are American couple." He nodded his approval. "Look nice together."

Sadie looked over at Calan, who looked at her. He recovered first.

"Thank you." He took the clear plastic bag with no markings on it and guided her out of the shop.

It took her a few moments to stop thinking about how they looked together. Was it obvious even to strangers how well they hit it off? And then their situation entered her thoughts and ruined the fanciful speculation.

Her stomach growled. And she was so tired. "Let's go get something to eat and find a place to stay for the night."

"Already done. The place to stay anyway."

He'd called that woman again. Odie or whatever her name was. She seemed to have access to an endless bounty of resources, hinting that there was much more to Calan's shady background than met the eye. He was part of some kind of organization that had deep pockets. The yacht he'd chartered, the private plane and now a place to stay in Montenegro. All were proof that money was not an issue.

The only thing she wanted to know was what kind of organization did he work for? What was its purpose? If his character was any indication, she'd lean toward the good rather than the bad, but hey, she'd been known to be wrong before…

He'd stolen money. He had a passport delicatessen in his duffel bag. He had a gun. And he didn't answer all her questions. Not because her questions annoyed him, but because he had secrets. These glaring signs didn't paint him a glossy picture. And yet, it was hard to think of him as anything other than an upstanding kind of man.

They walked side by side along the narrow stone path. Stone buildings with white mortar windows and wood trim lined the walkway. Such a romantic setting. She covertly looked at Calan. He was big but he moved with smooth, sure strides, and his big hands held most of her bags.

"Do you think we look like husband and wife?" she asked.

"He was just trying to make a bigger sale."

"That's a typical guy answer."

"All he had to do was look at your ring finger."

She crowded him as other people passed coming the opposite direction. "Just because a girl doesn't wear a ring doesn't mean she isn't married."

She had to move closer to him again as a man rode by on his bicycle. "I think he really thought we looked married."

"Well, we aren't."

She caught the tense set of his mouth and realized he wasn't bored. He just didn't want to talk about it. What was it with him?

The cluster of old, white stone buildings complimented the city's twenty-five hundred year history and diverted her attention for a while. They emerged from the passageway and she caught a glimpse of the shimmering waters of the Adriatic Sea in the distance, and above the roofline of the other buildings, she could see the historic bell tower from here. If only this were a vacation instead of the colossal mess it was.

At the rental car, Calan opened the door for her. She slid onto the seat and put the bag in the back with the others.

What had caused that change in him? He didn't like talking about marriage. Maybe he was in a relationship gone sour? Was that related to his disenchantment with the military? She dared not to ask. Not now.

Rummaging through the shopping bags on the bed, Sadie dug out something comfortable to wear to bed. She'd just taken a shower and felt like a new woman. Earlier, they'd eaten an Italian seafood dish Calan had gotten from a restaurant on the way here. She'd devoured everything on her plate. She probably should just go to bed now, but everything that had occurred since yesterday was a jumbled knot in her head. She needed more relaxation.

Finding a long T-shirt that Calan had eyed in the clothing shop as if he preferred something sheer, she slipped it on and headed for the door of the room. With her hand on the door handle, she hesitated. What if he was still awake?

She was so at odds with her teetering emotions about him. The nagging inclination that she stayed with him by choice wouldn't leave her alone. Was she repeating the same mistake and making bad decisions? If she really wanted to get away from him, she could. She could at least try, anyway. She hadn't even done that. Not with any great determination. It was he who kept her at his side, and that was disconcerting to say the least.

Opening the door, she listened. It was quiet. Leaving the room, she walked down the hall from the master bedroom, which was at the end of the hall. Instead of a ramshackle place to hide for God only knew how long, Odie had found them a cozy, newly constructed villa. Comfortable. Nice. She could almost pretend they were on vacation.

She passed the room Calan had claimed, hoping he was in it and she could have some alone time. Emerging into the living room, she spotted him sitting on the couch. He'd just put his cell phone on the coffee table and now looked at her.

True to her torn heart, she walked over pale red floor tiles that stretched to a wall of windows adjacent to the kitchen as if a magnet drew her to him. Her bare feet sank into a contemporary and colorful rug that accented the white leather sectional where he sat.

He watched her approach. An increasingly familiar warm glow expanded the closer she came to him. Sitting on the couch, she caught his pleased but questioning gaze.

"Not tired?"

"Oh, I'm tired. Just too wound up for sleep."

"Me, too."

While he turned on the television and began surfing the channels, she checked the windows. Off the blue, yellow and red dining area, a door led to a sprawling balcony and windows covered most the wall. All the blinds were closed.

Earlier, she'd seen a pathway that wound its way between their villa and the one next to it and wondered if it led to the coast. Calan had told her the villa had a view of the sea. She'd love to take a long walk in the morning but doubted they'd have time. She didn't want the wrong people to see them, either.

Leaning back against the couch, she watched the channels change with each press of Calan's thumb. Tourist channel, weather, an old movie in a foreign language.

"What if Murati doesn't return?"

"He will."

"What if someone gets to him first?"

"They won't."

Rolling her head against the back of the couch, she looked at him. "Do you think he's involved with whomever is after you?"

He stopped surfing to return her look. Yeah, yeah, she was asking questions again.

"Is there a ferry that leaves from somewhere near here?" she asked just to be annoying.

He resumed surfing.

"I'm sure we could find one," she said.

"I'm sure we could." He sounded sarcastic.

"I don't understand why you think someone would follow me home." The only thing she was sure of was that he had a deeply personal reason for not wanting her to go home.

He stopped surfing to look over at her again. "You're staying, so don't argue about it anymore."

"I'm not arguing. I'm just saying, no one would follow me home if I took a ferry to Italy and went home."

"You don't know that for sure."

"Neither do you," she countered.

"You'd travel home with a fake passport?"

She looked away, unable to keep her uncertainty from showing. "I don't want to but I will."

"You want to get away from me that bad?"

She lifted her head off the back of the couch and didn't know what to say. She wanted to be with him, but not like this.

Leaving the TV on a travel channel, Calan leaned forward and put the remote down on the coffee table. "You're staying."

"Why are you so worried?" Somehow she'd get him to talk.

"They're going to assume you know about the money."

She decided to go along with his reasoning for a little longer. Maybe something would compel him to tell her the truth. "So? If I leave without it, they have no reason to come after me."

"Even if they knew you didn't take it with you, they'll

assume you know how to find me. And when they can't find me, where do you think they'll go for answers?"

"You're that sure they won't find you?"

He looked back at her from his slightly forward position on the couch in silent answer.

Did he think he was that good? "They found out you were at the embassy with me."

That reminder cleared some of his overconfidence. He didn't know who he was dealing with and until he did he had no way of knowing what they were capable of.

No more tap dancing. It was time to get to the point. "Why is it so important to you that I stay?"

After meeting her eyes for several seconds, he sighed and she saw him relent to something, some thought or knowledge that he'd kept from her until now.

"There has to be a reason," she persisted, leaning forward like him to bring her face closer to his. "You're concerned for my safety, but more than that is driving you."

As he blinked, a shield vanished to reveal resignation filled with sorrow. He was going to tell her.

She dared not move or say anything, just let him take his time to form thoughts into words, thoughts she could feel were deeply rooted and painful to bring to the surface.

"I've been after a man for a long time," he finally said. "For years."

"Who?"

"A terrorist."

Given all that had happened, his revelation came as no great surprise. "Why were you after him?"

"He was hard to track," he said as if she hadn't asked the question. "Every time I found out where he was, he always disappeared before I caught up to him. But not this time. This time I found him."

"In Tirana."

He nodded a couple of times. "I followed him to an old warehouse. He met with two other men who gave him the money in the suitcase. I couldn't take the chance of not catching him again, so I did what I came here to do and took the money."

"He was the target you talked about with Odie?"

Again he nodded, and she knew without asking that he'd killed the man. The idea should bother her, but it didn't. A terrorist wasn't an ordinary man. A terrorist was someone whose warped ideologies made him evil.

"His name was Abu Dharr al-Majid," he said. "Anyone giving him money means it was going for an illicit purpose. Terrorism. He had to be stopped."

So he hadn't really stolen the money. "I thought you said you weren't a bounty hunter."

"I'm not."

"Do you work for the government?"

He hesitated. "No. Dharr was a special circumstance. I've waited a long time to see him dead. An opportunity came up that helped me do that."

Special circumstance? An opportunity? Years he'd been after this man. One man. One terrorist. She was getting closer to peeling back the layers and finding the core of what drove him. "You must have really wanted to get him."

His face grew stony.

"What happened? What did he do?"

While he didn't respond, thoughts bombarded her. He didn't work for the government, so he'd come here unofficially. He had a personal vendetta with a terrorist. How had all that come to be? When had he crossed paths with such a man? Had he been somewhere during an attack? Or had his profession led him to this point? What had led him to work in the shadows?

"What are you going to do with the money?" she asked as a roundabout way to get her answer and to give him time.

"Give it to my employer."

"Who is your employer?"

He raised his brow with a gently admonishing look. "This is when I tell you to stop asking questions."

She paused awhile, and then asked as gently as she could, "What made this terrorist significant?"

"We had a mutual friend." Turning away, he picked up the remote and started surfing channels again.

It was time to start pushing. "Was it someone in your family?"

"No more questions."

"You never want me to ask questions. I could ask you if you have all ten toes and you'd skirt the issue." She was so sick of that. "You need to start telling me things. You owe me that much. None of this is my fault. I wouldn't be here if it weren't for you. I'd be at the hotel waiting for my passport...my *real* passport."

He stopped surfing. Leaning back against the couch, he stared ahead for a while. Her heart expanded with sympathy for him. She could feel his turmoil.

Finally, he turned to look at her.

"A long time ago, a friend of mine called and told me about a man who was holding a woman against her will. I owed him a favor, so when he asked if I'd go get her, I agreed." He stopped and she watched the pain of memory wrench him.

She leaned back against the couch with him and slid her hand onto his thigh.

"It happened when I was still with the Army Delta Force," he continued. "We stopped in Istanbul on the way to the location of our next assignment. That's when I got the call. The woman who'd been abducted was his sister. When I met him to get the details, he told me the man who kidnapped her was her boyfriend. When she tried to end the relationship, he wouldn't let her go."

Realization slammed into her. "Her boyfriend was Dharr?"

He didn't answer. He didn't have to.

"You rescued her?"

"Yes."

"Why didn't you kill him back then?"

"He didn't get in my way. I rescued the woman without incident."

She was missing something. "Then, why did you go after him after you rescued her?"

"After my assignment was finished, I had a few weeks off. I went back to Istanbul and stayed with my friend. I wanted to see his sister again. I spent every day with her while I was there. When I returned home, we had a long-distance relationship for a while, and then I helped her come to the States. A year later we were married."

He married her.

"Dharr didn't know about us at first," he said. "But somehow he learned she wasn't in Istanbul anymore. That's when he went to her brother and found out she was with me in the States."

He stopped.

"What happened?"

Calan leaned forward and turned off the television. "Three months after he discovered I married her, he found a way into the U.S. and killed her."

Sadie drew in a breath. "Oh, I'm so sorry." She really was. "That must have been terrible."

"That was more than seven years ago."

It had taken him that long to catch Dharr? "Have you been looking for him all that time?"

"Yes, every spare moment I had. But he was good at hiding. Moving around. Like a regular Bin Laden. I was on assignment most of the time. Sometimes that put me where I needed to be to track him and other times it didn't. I came close to killing him once when I tracked him to Yemen. I wasn't on assignment then, but I caught him in the middle of intercepting another special forces team. They didn't know he was there. It was a setup. I could tell the moment I saw him, hiding in a vehicle while his men swarmed a building where soldiers were waiting for rebels. The team was supposed to help the Yemen government, but someone betrayed them and told Dharr where they'd be. I tried to save them, but I was too late and I was only one man. I took down a few of Dharr's men but not in time. Dharr got away."

"Why did Dharr want American soldiers dead? Was it just because they were American? Who would tell him the location of U.S. soldiers?"

His hesitation and the way he averted his eyes revealed a lot. There was more.

"Years after my wife died, I met a woman who worked intelligence for the CIA. She helped me uncover an arms deal a U.S. broker was arranging for Dharr. The broker arranged for a U.S. senator to bribe an executive he knew at an Albanian military export company to do business with Dharr. Kate must have been close to uncovering that because she was murdered shortly after I told her what I knew about Dharr. It gave her the lead she needed to expose the senator."

One that led to her death. Her heart ached for him. "He killed two women you were involved with?"

His face became a mask of indifference.

"Is that why the soldiers were killed? They knew about the arms dealing?"

"Yes. One man on the team did."

One man had known something and all of them had been killed. A bonus package for a group of terrorists.

Dharr had killed all those people. His wife, the soldiers and then a woman who'd tried to help him. It was overwhelming. She couldn't imagine how difficult that must have been for him. And probably still was. "What happened with the senator? Did you know he and an arms broker were doing business with Dharr?"

"No, I didn't know. No one did, not in time anyway. Anyone who got too close to putting it together was killed. The senator didn't murder anyone, but he alerted Dharr, which in my mind is the same as committing the crime right along with him."

Except not in his wife's case. "Did you go to Kate because you knew she could help you?"

"No. I met her because we knew the same people within the military. The senator was her stepfather."

Sadie gasped. What an awful thing. Quite a coincidence, too, but Sadie didn't believe in coincidences. The senator was working with the terrorist Calan was after and neither he nor Kate had known. But their joining together had exposed the senator and led to Calan finding Dharr. Talk about divine intervention. Or just plain rotten luck. His probing had gotten another woman killed.

"Was the senator caught?" she asked.

"Yes, but he killed himself before he was arrested. The arms deal fell through, and Dharr got away."

Until he'd found him in Albania, ending years of anguish. Or not. How could any man put something so terrible behind him?

"I don't blame you for wanting him dead," she said and

was amazed that she meant it. How strange, to be talking about killing someone and not finding it in the least unwarranted.

He didn't seem happy about it, though, as if killing Dharr hadn't been enough. It hadn't brought Kate back. Or his wife.

She almost didn't want to ask. "Were you close to Kate?"

"We were living together."

Living together but not married.

"We talked about getting married."

Talked about it but never made plans.

"She wanted to, but I wasn't over Rachel yet," he said.

The scars he carried from losing his wife were too deep. He'd never stopped loving her and couldn't marry another until he could put it behind him.

"I should have married her, though. It hurt her knowing why I hesitated," he continued.

She saw his pain, the pain of regret, the worst kind.

"You loved her."

He nodded. "Yes. And I would have married her."

"I'm so sorry, Calan." Twice he'd fallen in love and twice that love had been ripped from him. "How long ago did she die?" she asked, even though it bothered her. She was falling for a man whose heart belonged to two other women.

"It's been six months."

Sliding her hand off his thigh, Sadie struggled with disappointment. That wasn't very long. He'd loved his wife and, later, his girlfriend, but both of them had been murdered. Taken from him in the worst possible way. By a terrorist's hand. She couldn't imagine how awful that must be.

Now more than ever she understood why he couldn't let her go, why he had to protect her at all cost. But it wasn't necessary. She knew that now.

"You have a good reason to be concerned for my safety, Calan, I can never argue that. But you're overreacting because of your past."

"I'm not overreacting."

"My father is a wealthy man. He can protect me."

"Would he?"

That stopped her. She looked down. The truth was, she didn't know what her father would do. He wanted her to grow up and handle her problems on her own. He'd left her in Albania for that very reason. And he might not even believe her if she told him what had happened since she'd last spoken with him.

She'd met a man who had killed a terrorist and taken money. The terrorist's business associates were after him, had seen her with him, and she was now embroiled in his situation. Would her father believe her? It was so different from her other situations. Much more dangerous. Far removed from the social scenes she frequented. She didn't think her own father would abandon her, not once she convinced him the most outlandish story she'd ever told him up to this point was true.

"Even if he did try to protect you," Calan said, "he won't have enough experienced men to do the job, and the police won't be able to do much. The feds, either, since I'd have to deny everything."

Because he couldn't talk about his current profession? He'd told her personal things, but when it came to what he did for a living he wasn't talking.

"Who are you?" She'd asked it before and hadn't gotten the answer she sought. She didn't think she'd get an answer now, but she was too baffled not to say anything.

"Just an ex-Delta soldier trying to do the right thing."

Just? It was more than she expected to hear. "But you aren't with the Army anymore."

"No."

"Is the company you work for legitimate?" She didn't want to find out he was a mercenary or some kind of extremist.

"The company I work for doesn't exist."

That was sort of like saying he wasn't wearing underwear when he really was. But his face showed no sign of mischief. He appeared completely justified in what he said. Righteous, but not in an egotistical way.

"I've already told you too much."

She smiled. "Thank you."

"Are you going to stop asking questions now?"

She didn't miss how he made light of something serious. "Funny, no one's ever told me I ask too many questions."

"Maybe you haven't had a reason to ask them until now."

But she did with him. "I've never been with anyone who worked for a company that doesn't exist but allows him to go after terrorists."

He didn't smile at her sarcasm.

She plopped back against the couch. "Maybe that's my problem. I try to please my dad by choosing friends I think he'd like."

He leaned back the same as her. "What would you want to do with your life if your father wasn't wealthy?"

That made her stop and think. "I don't know." She thought some more. "I suppose get a job like everyone else. Maybe open an art supply store. I like to paint, but I'll never be good enough to have my work in a gallery." Even saying it made her feel like she was shooting in the dark. "My parents never asked me what I wanted to do when I grew up. It was just assumed that I'd follow in my dad's footsteps."

"He wants you to run his company?"

"Some day, after he retires. It's the same thing you hear all the time. I feel like I'm playing a part in a rerun. The business tycoon expects his child to take over his empire but the child has other aspirations." Whatever those were. "Now my father's company will go to someone outside the family, which disappoints him immensely. It's caused a huge rift between us. Not that we were ever close. I was always running away from his lecturing. And I don't think he's ever forgiven me for not going to college."

"Sounds like you're trying too hard."

What did he mean? "I don't think I can try hard enough to please my father, not unless I do what he wants and agree to work at his company and work my way up to running it."

He put his arm along the back of the couch. "You don't pursue your art because your father doesn't approve."

His strong arm behind her distracted her and she had to remember what he'd said.

She did pursue her talent for art. She'd sold some prints at a county fair. Was he diminishing that like her father had? Her defenses reared up. "Just because my work isn't in a fancy gallery somewhere doesn't mean it isn't serious enough."

"I didn't say that."

"I never expect to impress my father with anything I paint and he never is."

"Did you hear yousrself when you said you weren't good enough to have your work in a gallery?" he asked.

He wasn't making fun of her work at all. He was encouraging her. Oh, she didn't want to feel this way with him. He made it worse by brushing back a few strands of hair that had fallen alongside her face. No one had ever supported her like this.

"Stop deliberately selecting people you think will fit the mold of what a friend should be. That's what I mean about trying too hard. If you meet someone, let it happen. They'll either be your friend or not."

Her skin was tingling even after he lowered his hand. "Yeah, and then they find out my father is rich and suddenly I'm no longer a person, I'm a bank account."

"Not everyone would be that way."

"Well, I have yet to meet them, then."

"You met me."

His blue eyes watched her and she melted into them. "Don't you care about money?"

"Of course I do."

But he didn't want hers. This was probably where her father would caution her to be careful.

"People have told me that before," she said, feeling her father coaching her. "That they thought I was special and it had nothing to do with my money." Or more appropriately, her father's money. She got up from the couch and walked to the window, opening the blinds to stare out at the darkness, dots of lights sparkling along the coastline.

She heard him approach behind her and lean so that his mouth was beside her ear. "I prefer to make my own way in life."

Turning, she backed away from him. "You can't tell me that you wouldn't like to find a woman who had money." Any normal person would want to land on a lot of money.

"I wouldn't care if she had money or not."

Why not? "Are you loaded or something? Do you make a lot of money?"

"I make a decent living."

Working for a secret company killing terrorists? "But not a lot?"

"What's a lot to you?"

She shrugged. She'd never really thought about it. "I don't know. A million or two a year would be enough." Did she sound as blasé as she thought she did?

"I think the cost of a new home is a lot. The cost of a college education is a lot. Starting your own business costs a lot. It's all about perception. For me, it isn't important that a woman I'm interested in has a lot of money, whether I'm *loaded*, as you put it, or not."

Realizing she'd probably offended him, Sadie berated herself. "I'm sorry. I have no tact." She was always doing that, forgetting her boundaries or the boundaries of others. She didn't want to offend Calan. She wanted him to like her, more than she'd ever wanted anyone to like her. And that spelled disaster. The last thing she needed was to try too hard to make him like her, a man still grieving the loss of two woman he loved.

No wonder everyone ran away from her. Well, maybe it was time for her to do the running.

Chapter 5

Feeling melancholy, Sadie went to the balcony door off her bedroom and walked outside, leaving the door open. Putting her hands on the rail, she smelled the sea air. It was a clear, warm night. She wished her head was clear.

Calan had opened her eyes to so many things and in such a short time. Having an open mind about his attitude over money probably wasn't good for her, though. He had a healthy attitude. An attitude she hadn't seen in anyone she'd met. Not genuinely. He'd also thrown a wrench into her perception of her artwork. She loved to paint. She felt grounded when she painted. It was her secret escape. But now she wondered if her father's disdain had kept her from pursuing a serious career. She'd set the bar too low for herself as a result. Selling at the county fair wasn't something to totally overlook, but what if she *could* do better?

Why shouldn't she explore her painting talent? She'd

never know how far she could go unless she tried. Really tried. She hadn't given her art her full effort. She could do more. And she didn't need approval from anyone.

If she got nothing more from her father's abandonment than that liberating realization, she'd be happy. Because her father *had* abandoned her by leaving her in Albania. And now that she thought of it, he'd abandoned her long before this. He'd abandoned her as soon as she showed a tendency toward the arts rather than math and science in grade school. He wanted a businessperson for a child. Sometimes she wondered if he wished she had been born a boy. Her mother had been unable to have more children. It amazed her that he'd stuck by her all these years. In public they never showed signs of affection. Sadie never saw them interact that way at home, either. Maybe a few times, but it was forced and seemed as though they'd both fallen out of a role.

A sound from beyond the far end of the balcony made her stiffen and jump. When she saw a shadow move beyond the railing, she managed to smother a loud yell.

One strong arm hooked her waist and a warm whisper came against her ear.

"Don't move."

Calan. He'd come through the door off the dining area, not her bedroom. She relaxed but only enough to stop from kicking him and fighting to escape.

He let her go and went to the far side of the balcony in his underwear, a gun drawn. She frantically looked around, panicked that perhaps whoever was lurking in the night might sneak up on her.

Rubbing her arms, she ignored Calan's directive not to move and went inside the villa. Standing in the dining room, she peered through the glass door, trying to catch sight of him through the darkness.

"I told you not to move."

She all but jumped out of her skin. Turning, she saw Calan standing there. He must have come through the balcony door off her room. Catching her breath, she looked through the glass door again. "Is he gone?"

"Are you sure it was a man you saw?" he asked. "Did you get a good look at him?"

"No." She began to grow aware of him in only his underwear. He'd put his gun away, though. Must have done that before coming back into the dining area.

"It was probably someone just walking by. There's a trail that goes between this building and the one next to it."

"I saw it, too."

He looked at her as if he appreciated her observation of that detail. His gaze touched her mouth and then met her eyes again. He didn't move and neither did she. She felt the energy shift, a living thing in the silence of the villa, so late at night.

"We should go to bed," she said before thinking.

He stepped closer.

"I mean, I didn't mean, I—I…"

He reached his hand behind her head and sank it into her hair.

Oh, God.

"I know what you meant." With that, he kissed her.

While a frenzy of arousing sensations mounted in her, she wondered if she'd be an idiot to explore this. He'd lost two women he loved to tragedy, and the second one hadn't been very long ago. He hadn't had enough time to heal.

Ending the kiss, she pushed his chest.

He released her with prowling eyes. He wanted her, that was clear. No man had ever looked at her like that. It kept her pulse going strong.

Get away from him.

Tripping over her own feet, she started to leave the kitchen. "I'm going to…I'm just gonna…"

She bumped into a kitchen chair and stubbed her toe. "Ouch!"

Limping around the chair, she made it into the living room.

"Are you okay?" he asked.

Hardly. Her toe was minor compared to the temptation blazing inside her.

At the hall, she looked back. He saw her hesitation and fire renewed in his eyes. Temptation circled stronger. She couldn't fight it and the sight of that bare chest didn't help. He started toward her. She took one step backward, her body clamoring for something sinful.

He reached her. When she felt his heat, she parted her lips for more air and tipped her head back a little. He put his fingers through her hair again, holding her head as he had before and kissing her as he had before. She melted into the play of their mouths. Sensation assuaged a burning need. She didn't want to end it.

Breaking away, she stepped back again. He radiated sexual hunger. The sight of him swept her further from reason.

They stood frozen for a few seconds, powerful energy electrifying a physical connection. That same chemistry she felt when she'd met him exploded now.

She moved at the same time he did. She landed against him, throwing her arms over his shoulders while his arms went around her and his mouth crushed hers for a deep, needy melding.

She whimpered and he groaned. When he began to walk, she wrapped her legs around him until he reached the bed in her room. He dropped her on the mattress and followed her down, kissing her more and tugging her T-shirt up over her head. He tossing it to the floor.

She slid his underwear over his hips and he finished removing them. When she opened her legs, he kneeled between them. The tip of him pressed against her and in the next instant he slid deliciously inside her. He didn't spend any time touching her anywhere else. He didn't kiss her. He just began thrusting. Deep and hard, reaching a sweet spot with each one that made her dizzy with passion. She pressed her hands against the wall, which made his thrusts more forceful. The friction and the full, hammering penetration drew up a cry from her. Her orgasm made her writhe with pleasure. She wasn't even aware of his, but as she floated back to coherency, she felt his weight on top of her and he was spent and catching his breath along with her.

Sadie stared up at the ceiling, stunned by the power of their joining. But she was afraid of what it meant to him. He'd lost two women he loved, the second not very long ago. How could this mean more than what it appeared—just a plain ole hankering for sex. She wasn't even sure she expected it to mean more than that. The only thing she was sure of was that she didn't want to feel more for him than he felt for her. That was a guaranteed path to a broken heart.

So what was this, then? She'd never had a just-sex relationship before and she didn't want to start one now.

Feeling cheap and sleazy, she pushed against him. "Get off."

Calan lifted his head and looked at her, confused. "What's the matter?"

She shook her head, rolling it on the pillow.

"Are you hurt?"

"No." A stifled sob escaped. "This doesn't mean anything to you."

"What?"

"It was sex."

Silence answered her.

It was enough. Sadness and self-disgust consumed her. She sniffled, fighting a fresh and much more earnest wave of tears.

"Sadie."

She didn't want to look at him.

He cupped her face and made her. Her vision blurred with tears, but she saw raw sincerity in his gorgeous eyes.

"I can't promise you anything right now, but this was more than sex to me," he said. "I wouldn't have done it otherwise."

So this wasn't a one-time thing. That didn't reassure her. It still didn't mean enough to him. It couldn't. They'd have a fling for a while and then it'd be over when it came to the point when he couldn't give her what she needed. She'd made the wrong decision again, a mistake, a bad choice. Like she always did. She was always misjudging people, giving everything when they weren't in a place to give as much in return. She had believed in others and they had turned their backs on her. There would come a day when he'd do the same.

When was she going to learn?

"Sadie."

She opened her eyes, only just then realizing she'd closed them. Her heart broke looking at his handsome face.

"This wasn't a mistake." He pressed a soft kiss to her mouth. "It means more than that."

There was no point in discussing it. His losses were too great. Talking about them and how they measured up to this would be futile. This didn't measure up to that. But she kissed him to make him believe she was fine. He hesitated but then relaxed.

When he rolled off her, she curled next to him, moving

her head to see his face without alerting him. Seeing him staring at the ceiling, she knew he'd only been trying to make her feel better. He wasn't sure where this would lead. He could make no promises. He'd said as much, hadn't he? This might not be a mistake for him, but it was for her. She shouldn't have allowed this to get as far as it had. He might be able to walk away from something casual, but she didn't do casual. Not with him. Not with the way she felt for him.

Calan woke to his cell phone ringing. Half sitting up, he glanced over and saw Sadie beside him and the rush of memory staggered him for a second. Arousal collided with uneasiness. When his phone rang again, he picked it up and answered, pushing covers aside and getting off the bed.

He cleared his throat. "Yeah."

"What is it, nine there?" Odie goaded.

"About that."

"You sound like you just got up."

He had a feeling he was about to suffer one of Odie's infamous episodes of probing into personal matters that were better left alone. "What have you got for me?" When he'd called to ask her to find them this villa, he'd also asked her to look again into Murati's background, as well as that of Arber Andoni, the owner of the airport who may have had ties to Dharr.

"Late night, huh?"

"Just tell me what you have."

She laughed lightly. "I shouldn't do this…having been on that end of things, but…I can't resist…you slept with her, didn't you?"

He sighed and looked at Sadie, whose eyes had opened and, though drowsy, weren't happy. When her gaze dropped to his nakedness, apprehension gripped him. He should have never allowed this to happen. A brief affair was fine by him, but the woman he shared that with had to be looking for the same thing. Sadie wasn't, and that made him feel as if he'd crossed a line he couldn't revoke. He didn't understand how it could have been so easy to fall into bed with her. Why hadn't he thought about the morning after? About how Sadie would feel. Maybe he thought—or hoped—she knew what she was getting into. Maybe she had, but like him, it hadn't mattered. But it did now.

"What is it with you guys?" Odie brought him back. "It seems like you find a damsel on every mission. Is it part of the job description?"

He turned his back to Sadie. "When you're finished entertaining yourself, will you let me know what you found out?"

"You're no fun, are you? All right, I'll go easy on you. I found nothing new, that's what I found."

Calan put on his underwear, holding the phone between his head and his shoulder. They'd bribed Murati to arrange for them to fly into Andoni International Airport. They'd paid a lot of money to avoid identifying the company that employed them and their reason for coming to Albania.

"Arber Andoni and Armend Murati both still check out, beyond what we already know about them. Whoever they're working with is real good at staying under the radar."

Either that or they hadn't recognized the connection yet. Andoni allowed illicit transport through his airport for a price but he wasn't dealing himself, and Murati took bribes. But either one of them, or both, was working with someone who'd intended to do business with Dharr.

"Murati could have told Andoni about you," Odie said. "And if Andoni knew Dharr..."

"Yeah. I'll find out as soon as I talk to Murati."

"You going to take your baggage with you?"

Baggage. There was a word. He heard Sadie move on the bed behind him. He looked back at her. She sat up on the mattress, holding the sheet up over her chest. "I don't think I have a choice."

"You could send her home. We could have someone meet her."

"I took the equivalent of three million dollars, Odie."

"Yeah, you did. She didn't."

"You know how these things work."

"Yes, and I also know why you don't want her out of your sight. We could protect her on this end, and you know it."

"I'll get back to you when I know more." He wasn't going to get into that discussion with her. Before she could say more, he disconnected and turned around.

"Get dressed," he told Sadie, irritated. Whether Odie was right or wrong, he wasn't going to risk another woman's life.

Her brow furrowed. "Good morning to you, too."

Last night when she'd started crying, he'd been as honest as he could have been. The only thing left unsaid was that he'd loved twice in his life and didn't think he had it in him to love a third time, nor did he believe he'd get that lucky again. Not with the memory of Kate still so fresh in his heart and soul…

Leaving the room, he went to shower in the other bathroom.

Odie's subtle reminder that everyone at TES knew why he'd joined the team pulled his mood down. It made him think of Kate. He missed her witty intelligence. Her big smile and the sound of her laugh. She was always positive. And yet, she had a hard side, the CIA side of her. When push came to shove, she was a formidable opponent. But when it came to matters of the heart, he'd never met anyone capable of so much warmth and selfless love.

She hadn't deserved to die the way she had. Finding her had nearly killed him. He'd left after a fight they'd had over details surrounding Dharr and had come home to find her with her throat slit. He should have never left her. He should have believed her, too. And not argued. One thing Kate had been really good at was deciphering the information she gathered.

A lead had been planted to throw them off and he hadn't believed her when she'd figured it out. She'd been right. He'd been wrong. Now she was dead and he'd never be able to apologize.

The look on Calan's face when he'd left for his shower was still putting a crushing weight on her chest. Sadie stared at herself in the bathroom mirror. Last night he hadn't misled her over where this was headed. He'd confessed he couldn't make promises. But he'd also said what happened meant something. It did. She believed that. But it didn't mean enough. Physical attraction wasn't the only ingredient in a relationship.

"You have to stop being so stupid," she told her sad reflection.

Once again, she was glad her dad was never going to find out about this.

Disgusted, she got in the shower and let the spray hit her back. The morning after their magical night, Calan woke up thinking about the women he'd been with who'd died. It was plain on his face. She didn't have to be telepathic to know that. There was regret in his eyes. Regret and deep, gouging pain that comes with the loss of a loved one. His heart belonged to another. When it came time to go home, she'd never see him again.

She stomped her foot with a splashy thump.

Getting out of the shower, she dried off. Now she'd

have to go and face Calan. What if another situation arose that led to a repeat of last night? Would he want her to accommodate him again before this adventure was over? Would she have the wherewithal to stop him?

The more she ruminated over it, the angrier she became. After dressing, she went back into the bathroom to finish getting ready.

A loud crash made her jump. Glass shattering. She spun around in time to see two men with guns rush into her room. She screamed. Both were big men wearing black. One wore a hat. He hung back as the other man approached the bathroom, pointing a gun at her.

Sadie backed up against the bathroom vanity, frantically searching for an escape. Where could she go? What could she do? She was trapped.

The man charged forward, grabbing her by her elbow and yanking her out of the bathroom. She struggled to wrench free, but he jerked her toward him and looped his arm around her waist. She searched for some kind of weapon. Nothing was in reach. Then the man pressed his gun to her head. She stopped breathing and went still.

He hissed something in a language she didn't understand and then in English, "Do not move."

She didn't fight him, too aware of the hard, cold metal of the gun against her temple. That's when she saw Calan standing in the threshold of the room, aiming his gun at the man in the hat. His eyes shifted from her and the man who held her to the man in the hat.

She didn't want to die. Not yet. And not like this.

Calan walked toward them.

"Stop," the man in the hat said, his voice heavily accented.

Taking two more steps closer, Calan stopped, meeting Sadie's eyes. Was he gauging her, measuring her fear? She hoped he could tell that it was soaring. Or was he sending her some kind of message? What was he going to do? He had to know she was no good at this.

"Drop your weapon," the man in the hat said.

Calan looked at him. "Who are you?"

"Drop it, Mr. Friese."

They knew his name. His ties to Dharr had given that away. Calan didn't respond. His aim remained steady. If he fired his gun, the man in the hat would be shot. But the man holding her would get a shot off, too.

"I don't think I need to explain to you the consequences if you don't," the man in the hat added.

"Who are you? How did you find us?"

The man in the hat smiled without humor. He didn't have to answer, but he did. "It pays to have business acquaintances. We know many in the area. You were seen at the Afrodita Boutique. From there, it was easy."

It was already obvious that they were well-connected, but all the way into Montenegro? Just how far did their tentacles go?

"Tell me where the money is or she dies."

"Sorry. I can't do that."

The man's face hardened and he turned to her and the man who held her. Sadie saw Calan move his aim and felt his gaze pass hers to meet the man's who held her. Was he going to try a shot like that? It was too close! Oh, God. She was going to be killed!

"Calan!" she all but screamed.

"Kill her," the man in the hat said.

Sadie screamed, "No!" as Calan fired his weapon. The man holding her dropped, dragging her down with him. Another gunshot went off as she landed on top of the man and she realized it had been his gun. She didn't think she'd been hit. She didn't feel anything anyway. On her hands and knees over the man's limp form, Sadie came face to face with a dark red hole in his forehead and dead eyes staring at nothingness.

She screamed again, gutturally this time. Bile rose in her throat, made sicker by her heavy, horrified pulse. Scrambling off the dead man, she crawled backward like a crab, falling on her rear. Calan and the man in the hat were locked like wrestlers. She scooted out of the way when their brawling feet almost mowed her over. Calan broke his arms free and hit the man with the handle of his gun. The other man's hat went flying and he staggered back. But he managed to unsteadily swing his gun around.

Using that to his advantage, Calan chopped the man's wrist with an upward movement of his hand. The man still held his weapon. Calan jabbed his throat with the side of his hand before he could recover. The man doubled over and Calan rammed his knee upward, gripping the man's gun hand and squeezing. The man went to his knees. Calan pressed his gun to the man's forehead.

The man let go of his gun and Calan kicked it across the floor toward Sadie. Automatically, she lifted the gun. Standing, she aimed it and hoped she appeared threatening.

Calan banged the barrel of his gun against the man's head. "Who sent you?"

The man looked up at Calan with feral eyes, blood oozing from his nose and a cut on his lower lip.

"Who?" Calan repeated.

Sadie backed toward the door and stopped when she felt she was far enough away and close enough to the door to escape if she needed to.

"Kill me, more will follow," the man said, spitting blood onto the floor.

"Who sent you?"

The man continued to stare up at him in that eerie way. "Give me the money and no one else will come for you. It will end here. Now."

"No deal. Who sent you?"

After a momentary stare-down, the man dropped into a low roll. Springing to his feet from a crouch, he reached under the hem of his pant leg at the same time and his hand came up with a knife.

Calan fired.

The unexpectedness of it gave Sadie a jolt. Dropping the gun, she covered her mouth with a gag, looking away as a hole similar to the one in the other man appeared in the man's forehead.

Unaffected, Calan knelt before the man and began searching his clothes. He pulled something out, a business card. Next came a cell phone.

Not wanting to be in the room anymore, Sadie headed for the front door. She couldn't stay here anymore. She had to get away from all this violence. From the death. But most of all, from Calan. Facing his troubled past was one thing, but this was the final straw. Seeing those men killed had pushed her over the edge.

At the villa door, she grabbed the door handle and yanked. It didn't budge. She yanked and yanked and then realized the door was locked.

With shaking fingers, she unlocked the bolt.

Opening the door, it slammed shut before there was more than an inch or two of space. Turning, she leaned her back against the door and met Calan's intense face. His hand was still on the door above her head and she got a flash of déjà vu.

He'd done this at the hotel in Tirana, too. He wasn't going to let her go.

"Calan..."

All he did was shake his head.

There was no point in arguing with him, so she didn't. Not now. But when the right moment came, she was out of here.

Chapter 6

Sadie watched the streets of Budva pass by her passenger window. The sound of tires and air friction mixed with Calan's voice as he told Odie about the two men who'd broken into their villa this morning. Odie was asking a lot of questions.

"One had a business card with the name Gjergj Zhafa and an address in Tirana." Another pause ensued as the mysterious Odie grilled him again.

"A shop owner told him we stopped in his store," he said. "Whoever we're dealing with has a lot of friends. Will you get me what you can on Zhafa?" He paused. "Thanks, I appreciate that. I'll call you with status as soon as I have something."

He ended the call.

"Why do you keep calling her?" Was she his boss or something? "What is she, some kind of spy? Is that what you are?"

"She does intel."

Of course. Intel. And his answer was as brief as ever. "Must be some organization you work for."

"It has its freedoms."

Wouldn't he be free to go after terrorists on his own? Why did he need this organization? Protection? Secrecy? She decided to try and get him to talk more. "I thought it didn't exist."

"It doesn't."

He pulled to a stop near the boutique where they'd stopped yesterday. "Wait here."

Sadie glanced around the street. This could be a good opportunity to make her escape. There were ferries that left from Bar, which was down the coast from Budva, but she'd have to find her way there.

She looked over at the keys still in the ignition and then at him. He didn't have anything with him. If she drove off after he went inside, he'd be left here with nothing but a lot of dangerous men after him. He did have a gun…

Just when she began wondering where his passport was, he said, "On second thought, why don't you come with me."

She saw the way he was looking at her. She'd given away her thoughts. He'd seen her eyeing the keys. Getting out of the car, he walked around to the other side and opened her door.

"Come on."

"But…"

"Sadie, just come with me."

Reluctantly, she climbed out of the car. He slammed the door and she caught his reprimanding look. Ignoring that, she walked with him toward the narrow stone passageway that led to the boutique. The first time she'd walked this way, she'd enjoyed the sights. But even surrounded by pristine white stone architecture and Mediterranean red roofs, everything seemed darkly gothic to her now, like the set of a horror film.

"Stay close to me," he said.

As if he'd let her go anywhere else…

At the door of the boutique, Sadie saw there were lights on inside. Calan tested the handle and found it unlocked. From inside, exotic music sounded eerie in the otherwise-empty shop. He glanced at her and she saw his concern. It was still pretty early and the boutique shouldn't be open for a few more hours.

With another scan of the street, Calan entered and pulled out his gun. She stayed on his heels as he walked through the shop, jam packed with clothes and accessories. He checked the aisles and behind the checkout counter.

Sadie saw a door leading to the back at the same time he did. There was a light on back there, too, and the door was cracked open. She put her hand on his back as he approached the door, heart hammering.

Calan stopped and looked back at her as if the touch had distracted him. She dropped her hand.

He moved for the door again. There, he pushed it open a little bit farther and stilled. She saw what had made him stop so abruptly. He faced her and put his hands on her shoulders, pushing her back. But it was too late to keep her from seeing a man slumped in a chair with his arms tied behind the back. He was covered in blood and more pooled on the floor.

She fought a gag and put her face against Calan's chest. "No more. No more." She couldn't stand it.

He curved an arm around her. "Time to go. I don't want to be caught here."

No kidding. Outside of the boutique, he opened the car

door for her and she got in, putting her hand over her queasy stomach. Calan drove the car into the street.

"Why did they kill that man?" Three dead bodies in one morning was too much for her to endure. The images would be stuck with her forever.

"Maybe they thought he knew more than he did."

"About you?"

He hesitated. "Us."

She really wished he wouldn't say that. "How did they find us? That man didn't know, so why kill him? He was innocent."

"Maybe because he did business with us. Maybe because he couldn't tell them where we were staying. Who knows."

They killed because they could. She shuddered to think what kind of organization had that kind of ruthless power. *Someone must have seen us go into the boutique.* They were in Montenegro and still someone had recognized them.

"How did they find us at the villa?"

"I don't know. The shop owner may have given those men a description of our car. They may have had a lot of help asking around."

A lot of help…

How could Calan expect to be able to do anything against a group like that? He was outnumbered, for one thing. And these men were dangerous. It was too much.

"I don't want to be here anymore." And for the first time, she really meant it.

At the desperate tone of her voice, Calan turned his head briefly.

"I want to go home."

"I'm sorry, Sadie. It's too late for that."

"You should have left me at the hotel in Tirana. I would have been fine. Guns and blood and people dying in front of your eyes might be nothing new to you, but it is for me. I can't do this!"

His mouth tightened and his jaw flexed. He didn't look at her, but his brow had lowered. She could feel his frustration. He didn't want to make her be here, but he felt he had to. She understood he had a good reason, but he had to see her side of it. Her side of it mattered. It was time for him to start facing that. It was time for him to start facing the fact that it was his past that influenced his actions when it came to her.

"Do you think I want another woman I've slept with to end up dead?" he finally said.

No, of course he wouldn't, but he might not be able to prevent it. A second later she realized the way he'd said that sounded as if he cared, more than she thought. It made her wonder if there was hope for them after they returned to the States.

"Please try to trust me a little," he continued.

She didn't answer because she wasn't sure she'd be wise to trust him. He may have good intentions, but those intentions might get her killed. Glancing over at him, taking in how clean-cut he looked in his short-sleeved white and thin, blue-striped, button-up shirt for what must be the hundredth time since they'd left the villa, she despaired. She didn't trust herself, either.

Sadie spotted the port as they entered Bar, Montenegro. She waited until after they passed before asking, "Can we stop somewhere so I can use a bathroom?"

He looked over at her as if trying to determine if she was going to try to run again. Of course he'd seen the port. He knew it was there. But he said, "Sure," and drove down the road until a gas station came into view.

It was an interesting gas station, with only a couple of

old pumps and a building that functioned as both gas station and a restaurant. Pulling in front of the building, Calan got out with her. She'd expected that. But instead of following her inside, he leaned against the driver's door and waited. Watching her all the way. He didn't comment on the fact that she'd taken her newly purchased handbag.

She entered the station. An attendant helped a customer at a small counter on one side of the store. On the other, and taking up most of the room, was a small restaurant. Straight back and nearest the counter, she spotted a single door down a hall. Passing a clerk who was still busy with the customer, she walked to the hall. At what must be the bathroom, she stopped. Down the hall was a back room. She looked behind her. The clerk had finished with the customer but had turned his back. She couldn't see Calan through the windows. The corner of the hall blocked her view.

Opening the door to the bathroom in case he could see the top frame, she closed it again without entering. Then she walked briskly down the hall. In the back room, a door was propped open as if to let the air in.

She left the building and looked around. Rundown houses backed to the station and other buildings along the road where she and Calan had driven. Running down the dirt alley, she made it to another busy street and started searching for a cab, searching also for any sign of Calan. It wouldn't take him long to start looking for her.

Minutes later she spotted a marked taxi and held up her hand. The driver pulled over. She got in and told him where to take her. Thankfully, he understood her English and she didn't negotiate the fare, just agreed on his price. A quick check through the rear window showed no sign of Calan.

She breathed a sigh and sat back for the short trip to the port.

After paying the taxi driver, she headed for ticketing on one of the ferry lines. Shortly thereafter, she discovered the soonest she'd be able to board was two days from now. Everything in her sank like an anchor. So much for planning her escape. She should have thought of that. Clearly, she needed more practice at this.

Feeling a good pout settle in, she found a seat on a bench near the entrance and waited for Calan…because she knew he'd be here soon. She didn't have to worry about that. She wouldn't spend much time here alone, and she wouldn't be stranded in Montenegro. She could depend on him for that.

A big, tall man entered the building. He was silhouetted against the light coming through the glass behind him, but she didn't have to see him in living detail to recognize him. She wasn't expecting him to be this fast.

He strolled toward her calm as could be. She hadn't been sitting five minutes. Even if there had been a ferry she could have caught, she doubted she would have made it on board. His long strides were unhurried and his eyes were hidden by sunglasses. But his mouth was in a familiar hard line as before and the way he moved would make anyone steer clear of him.

He stopped in front of her and just looked down at her, his head angled ever so slightly. She felt his angry smugness and a silent "Really?" all but hung in the air between them.

Sadie rolled her eyes and stood. "Don't say it." She started walking toward the exit.

He walked beside her. "First rule when trying to escape someone— Never tell them your plans."

Yes, she'd already recalled how she'd asked him to take her to the ferry, and she could kick herself for that as much as not checking ferry schedules first.

"Second rule— Always have a credit card that matches your false identification."

She hadn't even thought of that. She had cash for the ferry but not enough to buy a plane ticket. Feeling like an idiot, she said in her defense, "Well, it wasn't my choice to be dragged into this situation. I don't have the experience you do at this, and everywhere we go somebody ends up dead."

"Better them than us," he said.

She stopped and put her hands on her hips, getting mad now. "It could be us."

"Not if I can help it."

"You see? Even you aren't sure."

"Did you think you could just hop on a ferry and be sailing within the hour?" he asked.

It grated on her that he was rubbing that in.

"What were you going to do? Wait a few days? Where would you have gone?"

"I waited for you."

That made him hesitate. Now he knew she'd been well aware that he'd come for her and that it wouldn't take him long to find her.

"Guess I'll have to be more careful next time," she added.

"Don't waste your time, sweetheart."

His cocky sureness offended her. Didn't he think she could get away from him? Maybe she'd have to show him otherwise. She may have spoken before thinking and not planned ahead, but she knew better now. She had a good teacher.

When Calan pulled to a stop behind the short line of cars waiting to cross into Albania, Sadie was more nervous than ever. Not only was she using her fake passport again, she was going back to Albania, where people wanted them dead.

The line moved forward. So far the border officers hadn't held anyone up, despite the fact that border traffic wasn't busy today. There was only one car in front of the customs building.

A cyclist rode away from the booth after he was cleared and the car in front of them was next. The border officer inside the booth reached for papers the driver extended to him. Sadie looked around. Another border officer leaned against the stone siding of the customs building, smoking a cigarette. Another straightened from the window of the car that was parked there. The man inside backed away and drove toward the border patrol booth. All clear.

The customs building wasn't very big, one story high and maybe a hundred feet long. It had seemed bigger the first time she'd seen it, probably because she'd been so scared then. She was scared now, too, but having experienced crossing once before seemed to have desensitized her a little.

Calan pulled forward. It was their turn.

The officer took their passports and studied them.

"One moment," he said in accented English, turning with their passports and bending over a rear counter, looking at something there.

Sadie's heart sped up. It didn't help that Calan looked at her and she saw his concern. He wasn't so sure this time, not knowing how far-reaching Dharr's business associates were.

When the officer faced them again, he said, "Wait over there."

Not good. What had he checked? Was this another useless delay or had their names shown up on someone's radar?

Another officer, this one armed, waved them toward the customs building. Calan parked in front of it, not far from the entrance, and the officer who'd checked out the other car with the man inside approached. The armed officer handed him their passports. He looked at them and then bent to Calan's open window, glancing briefly over at Sadie. This time there was no interest in her legs. She'd worn jeans and a white T-shirt tucked in at the waist. Nothing feminine. Not that it would have worked anyway.

"Come with me," he said.

Starting to shake and feeling all the blood leave her head, Sadie walked with Calan toward the customs building. Glancing behind her, she saw that the other guard was searching their vehicle. Calan held the door for her and saw the guard searching their car rental, too. She shared a look with him and didn't like the worry she caught, however brief it had been.

Inside the building, the man led them past a small but open room with a single counter. A woman stood behind it, absorbed in some kind of papers there, a man standing before her. She glanced up but didn't pay them much attention.

Sadie watched Calan look around the room, along the ceiling, along the floor, behind the counter and at the woman. He took everything in.

The officer led them down a narrow, short hall to the first door on the right and then gestured for them to go inside.

"Is something wrong?" Calan asked before entering.

"Please wait here."

"Why are we being detained?"

"I do not know. We were instructed to keep you here for police questioning."

Police questioning.

Sadie felt faint.

Calan, however, didn't miss a beat. His hand slipped under his short-sleeved shirt and pulled out his gun. Snatching a fistful of the man's shirt, he pressed the barrel to his head and leaned close.

"Give the woman our passports," he said, sounding calm.

With round, fearful eyes and rapid breaths, the man began sputtering unintelligible pleas.

"Quiet or I'll pull this trigger."

With a tremble to his hand, the man kept his eyes on Calan while he handed the passports to Sadie.

She took them, gaping at Calan. "What are you doing?"

"If we stay here, we're dead." Then to the man, "Walk to our car. If anyone gets in our way, tell them to stop or I'll kill you."

Did he really think this was going to work? They'd take a hostage and drive away? They'd never get across the border alive.

"Calan."

"Be quiet, Sadie, and stay behind me. When we're outside, I'm going to get you to the car. I want you to get in the backseat and keep low. I'll do the rest."

"Oh, my God." She felt sick she was so scared.

"Do what I tell you, Sadie." He must see her fear. "You can't stay here. Do you understand me?"

Unsteadily, she nodded. She didn't want to stay here.

"Walk behind me."

He forced the man to walk back down the hall. They didn't encounter anyone on the way, but when they reached the entrance, the woman behind the counter dropped a stack of papers and her eyes widened. The man she'd been helping had already gone.

"Tell her to put her hands up and don't move. If she

doesn't do what you tell her, I'll kill you." He gave the man a yank. "Tell her in Italian so I can understand you."

The man spoke rapidly in Italian. The woman raised her hands and didn't move.

Sadie followed Calan through the front door, stark fear drying her mouth. The sun was dulled by a hazy sky. Their rental car wasn't far away. Everything was surreal.

A border officer stopped short as he walked toward the building.

"Tell him what you told the woman." He jabbed the man with the gun. "In Italian."

The man complied.

The officer was slow to raise his hands and Sadie watched him search around. The booth officer hadn't noticed them. But the armed officer searching their car did. He straightened as he closed the trunk.

"Tell him to get away from the car," Calan ordered the man he held at gunpoint.

The man did as asked. The armed guard hesitated.

"Tell him to drop his gun or I'll shoot you in the head."

The man sounded terrified as he translated to the other man, who slowly dropped his gun to the ground. The man at gunpoint was sobbing now.

Calan said something to the officer in Italian. The man kicked his gun so that it slid over the dirty ground.

"Sadie, pick up the gun."

Pulse charging full-out, she grabbed the gun. Crouching low, she moved closer to the car and with a shaky hand reached for the rear door handle. Her fingers slipped off the handle. She bit back an alarmed cry and gripped the handle again, fearfully searching for anyone who might shoot her. The door opened and she crawled into the backseat, dropping the gun on the floorboard and covering her head.

Calan slammed the door shut.

Slowly, she moved her hands down to the cushion of the seat and raised herself up a tiny bit. Peeking over the back of the seat, she saw the booth officer twist on his chair and see them. A couple in the car that had stopped at his window turned to look at them, too.

"Tell them all if they shoot at us or try to follow, I'll kill you. I have nothing to lose and you know it."

The man did as Calan said, having composed himself enough to raise his voice so the man in the booth could hear him.

Calan's dangerous gaze must have convinced him not to argue. He spoke to the other men, who didn't move.

"Good. Now get in and drive."

The man hesitated. Sadie saw his fear and wilted inside. This was so not her. She hated to see others suffer, even though she knew they'd be the ones facing death if they stayed.

"Drive," Calan repeated. "If you do what I say and we get across this border, I'll let you go."

The man looked around at the handful of men who aimed weapons at them but hadn't fired. Then he looked at Calan again.

"I have nothing to lose," Calan repeated.

The man met his gaze and saw what Sadie saw—a man willing to do anything to get across the border and die doing it.

The man got into the car.

Moving to the other side of the backseat to make room for Calan, Sadie stayed low, wondering crazily if a bullet would hit her through one of the windows.

Calan sat in the backseat and returned the gun to the

man's head. The man's eyes looked into the rearview mirror as he started the car and backed it away from the building. Men scurried in different positions, aiming guns. Two of them ran for a car, but a third stopped them, speaking urgently.

The officer drove past the border station booth, running over a wooden barricade blocking that lane. Sadie caught sight of the booth officer talking into a phone.

"Drive faster," Calan shouted.

The man sped the car up. Calan kept glancing behind them.

"They'll give us a little time, but they'll follow," he said to Sadie.

Great. Just what she needed to hear.

A few miles down the road, he told the driver to stop. He did.

"Get out."

The driver opened the door and got out, stumbling a little. He looked afraid as he stood by the car with his hands raised.

Calan checked him for weapons and took his pistol, tucking it into the front of his pants.

"Lay down on the ground, face down."

The man hesitated, but not for long. He did as ordered.

Calan got into the car and sped away. "Stay down."

Did he think she wouldn't?

He drove like a madman down the highway. Unbelievably, no one caught up to them. But how long of a reprieve did they have?

Chapter 7

Sadie stood before the rundown pension and marveled over the extent of disrepair. "Have you been here before?"

"No." Sounding insulted over why she'd asked, he headed toward the chipping front door.

"Is that a broken window?" She pointed to the third level, where it looked like someone had thrown a rock through the glass.

He looked up there. "I'm sure there are other rooms."

"Your friend Odie isn't a very good travel coordinator. How did she find this place?"

"The same way she found the passport place," he almost snapped.

He'd remained calm and patient until now. She'd gone at him most of the way here. After nearly being captured by nameless, faceless Albanian gangsters who had friends in Montenegro, she was getting low on tact.

"Did she find the airport you flew into, too?" The one

where his pilot had been murdered? She didn't say it because she didn't think she had to remind him.

He turned an exasperated look on her.

"I'm just saying..."

"We'll be safe here," he said curtly.

She'd refrain from believing that until *after* they checked out. He opened the chipping, creaking door and let her in before him.

The interior didn't disappoint. Sadie almost felt like whistling her acclaim. A stained rug might once have had a fancy mosaic pattern. She could barely make out the swirling grandeur of the blackened lines between shredding edges and ragged holes. The wood floor was missing pieces of planks and a layer of ground-in dirt covered them all. There were missing nails and nails that needed a hammer before someone cut their feet on them. On the wall, faded pictures hung in cluttered disarray.

A frail old man appeared through a filthy white door that didn't shut all the way but banged loud once and bounced off the frame, staying open about an inch. He smiled to reveal a few missing front teeth. His wiry gray hair hadn't seen a comb in a while and his dark skin was badly weathered.

Calan spoke to the man in Italian and soon he had a key.

"I feel safer already," she quipped and was rewarded with another vexed look.

He led her up a narrow stairway to the third floor. At the top of the stairs, he slid the key into a dark brown door. This room faced the back of the pension, so it couldn't be the room she'd seen from the front. She looked down the hall. Long rugs that were wrinkled and torn led to a window at the end, tall and filmy with sheer drapes that had once been white.

The last door on the right hung from one hinge. The room with a broken window.

Calan entered their room.

The worn, cracking and dirty tile floor was adorned with a round rug that was equally dirty and fraying badly around the edges. There were two twin-sized beds.

"Do you think the sheets are clean?" she asked.

Putting his duffel bag down, he ignored her and went to the window, parting the curtains.

Probably not.

"At least the glass isn't broken," she said, looking around the rest of the small room. There was no telephone and no television and…

"No bathroom?" She gaped at him.

"It's downstairs." He glanced back at her but returned to his study of whatever was outside the window. What was he looking for? More goons after the money he should have never taken?

"We have to share it?"

"Yes."

"Maybe I'll just go outside." A shrub had to be more sanitary than a toilet in this place.

Turning, he said, "It's only for a couple of nights."

"That's too long for me." She couldn't help it. Last night still grated on her. Maybe that's what made her so bratty right now. It was her defenses lashing out, clamoring for retaliation at the unfairness, even though the blame fell on her as much as him. He hadn't forced her to do anything. She'd made her own decision. Another bad one, true to her track record, but hers all the same.

After a time, he sighed and moved closer to her. "I don't like this any more than you do."

Did he know how that only sparked more rebellion in

her? "What, being stuck together? There's an easy solution to that."

"We aren't stuck together."

"Could have fooled me."

He had to know what she was eluding to. Last night. Having sex. Tonight was going to be a lot different. She was going to keep her distance. Not that she had to try very hard.

"I don't feel stuck with you," he said.

She put up her hands. "Let's not talk about it."

"Last night..." he hedged anyway. "I should have known better. I should have thought it through first. I didn't mean to..."

Make her believe she was different? That she mattered more than she actually did? "I'd rather just let it go."

"I wasn't thinking."

Rejection came in so many forms, didn't it? All she could do was stand there feeling the sting of his subtle but unmistakable retreat. He wished he'd never touched her.

"Neither was I," she said simply. She never did when it mattered. "We both made a mistake."

When his expression eased of tension, she knew she sounded convincing. She should be glad, but she wasn't.

This was going to be such a long night.

After foregoing a shower in that awful bathroom—she'd gone and checked and discovered filth beyond comprehension and a toilet that was little more than a porcelain-rimmed hole in the ground—Sadie waited for Calan to finish looking out the window where he'd kept vigil on and off since they'd arrived last night. He'd also checked the hall and gone downstairs and outside in the front, checking the street.

Looking over his shoulder, seeing she was ready, he

moved away from the window and stopped before her where she stood by the bed.

"You ready?" he asked.

"For what? More shootouts?"

After flashing a tolerant look, he reached into his duffel bag and dug out the pistol he'd taken from the border patrol officer.

She folded her arms. "Huh. Guess so."

Removing the magazine, he checked inside and reinserted it into the gun, tugging it to make sure it was in place, ignoring her.

"What are you doing?"

"You need to learn how to shoot."

She gaped at him while he stuffed the gun into the waist of his pants next to the other one and straightened his gray T-shirt over them.

"What makes you think I don't know how to use one?"

"It was a little obvious."

Was it?

"Let's go."

"No!" She folded her arms. "I don't want to learn how to shoot a gun."

He went to the door and waited, impatience brimming.

Sadie glowered at him. "Stop looking at me like that."

"Like what?"

"Like you're Adam Krahl." With that, she marched past him, her elbow and shoulder bumping him on her way through the doorway. Stomping down the stairs, she felt an unreasonable rise of emotion. Why should some special ops man matter? He wasn't even a legitimate special ops man. So they'd had promise-free sex one night. Every woman needed to know what that was like, didn't they? So they knew what to avoid? Now she did and she would never do it again. Lesson learned.

If she ever learned from her mistakes. It wasn't looking too good right now.

At the rental car, she stopped at the passenger door, waiting to hear the unlock mechanism, a lump in her throat. The fact that he wanted to teach her how to shoot a gun wasn't what bothered her. And while the intensity of her feeling alarmed her, there was nothing she could do to stop them.

Calan's tactical boots scuffing the gritty pavement told her he'd stopped behind her. She looked over her shoulder to see his somber face.

"I'm sorry," he said.

She faced the car. "Unlock the door." He was no different than any other man she'd gotten herself involved with. It didn't matter why they walked away, they just did. All she wanted to do was go home.

"Sadie..."

The sound of his voice only made her despair more. He didn't want to hurt her, but he had. She looked down at her hand on the door handle.

He curled his fingers around her arm and pulled her so that she had to let go of the handle and turn.

Then his arm slid around her lower back. She put her hands on his chest, not having the desire to push him away. He was being too sweet.

"I don't want to feel the way I do about you," he said.

Expanding warmth thickened her pulse. They both wanted each other but there were too many complications. Neither of them could separate the reality of bad timing from this inexplicable attraction.

"It confuses me," he added.

Because of his history. Because he felt guilty. Like he

might be betraying Kate. She didn't like that at all, but his honesty meant a lot.

"I don't want to feel the way I do about you, either," she said.

A small, lopsided grin lightened his mouth. "Then maybe I shouldn't teach you how to shoot a gun."

"Too late." She smiled through her emotions. Let him worry about what she'd do with a gun. He didn't have to know she'd never shoot one after today.

Sadie walked beside Calan along the street. He'd parked the rental in a parking lot not far from here. And now he kept looking behind them as they walked along the downtown street. Turning a corner, they walked some more. When they headed for a rougher part of town, she looked at him.

"I thought you were going to teach me how to shoot."

"I am. But first we need a new car. I don't want to be seen in the rental."

Neither did she.

He searched their surroundings. A car pulled to the side of the road and a man got out and headed for a small market, slipping his keys into his coat pocket. Calan took hold of her hand and tugged her with him after the man. Inside the market, Sadie wondered what he was doing as he stopped to inspect some cheese when the man did. Turning from the display, Calan bumped into him.

"Scusi," he said.

The man looked momentarily annoyed but returned his attention to the cheese as Calan turned away, taking Sadie's hand again.

Outside, he headed for the man's car. Only then did she realize he'd taken the man's keys. Plucked them right out of the man's pocket without him even knowing.

"Get in."

"You're going to steal it?"

"Get in, Sadie."

She looked around to make sure no one noticed them and got in. Either she was getting used to this or his confession about not wanting to feel something for her was confusing her the way it did him. She wasn't even all that scared. As long as no one was dying in front of her...

Tirana faded from her passenger window and an open, shrubby landscape took its place. The mountainous background was breathtaking under a clear blue sky.

"Did Odie find us a shooting range or something?" she couldn't resist asking.

This time he smiled a little at her sarcasm. "No. I didn't need Odie for this one. We'll just go somewhere out of town. I know a place."

As soon as he said it, he slowed and turned onto a dirt road that wound its way up a mountain. At a clearing among a forest of pine trees, he finally stopped.

Picking up a box of ammunition from the backseat, he opened the car door and got out. Following him away from their stolen car, Sadie saw him remove the also stolen gun from his waist.

He extended the gun to her.

"Is it loaded?"

"Of course it is. Just take it." He picked up her hand with his free one and placed the handle in her palm.

She had to curl her fingers around the handle to keep from dropping it as he pulled his hand away.

He pointed to a lever. "This will release the magazine." He did it for her and the magazine popped free of the handle.

"Can't I just fire it if I have to?"

"Take it out."

She pulled the magazine from the gun and saw bullets inside. They reminded her of what she'd seen yesterday.

"Put it back in."

She looked up at him and then shoved the magazine back into the gun, venting her frustration.

"You check it by giving it a tug." He moved closer and showed her with his fingers rubbing against hers, but she felt the firmness of the magazine.

"It's full but you can get one more cartridge in the pistol."

How could he tell?

"This is called the slide." He pulled the top of the gun back and she saw a cartridge appear in the opening, making room for one more in the magazine.

"Ah," she murmured.

When he released the slide, he pressed the magazine release and it snapped loose. She removed it.

He took it from her and bent to open the box of ammunition that he'd put on the ground and took out a cartridge.

"You load the magazine rim first. Like this." He showed her and then removed the bullet to hand it to her along with the gun.

She tried to push the bullet cartridge into the magazine, but it was stiff and difficult with her small fingers. He'd made it look so easy. Her fingers slipped.

"Hold it like this," he said, moving around her and placing the gun back in her hands.

She looked up and over her shoulder at him. He was all business now. He wanted her to learn how to shoot and that was all that mattered. He didn't care about her klutziness.

"Use both hands and keep the barrel down."

Warmth edged its way through her core. He was a good teacher. Patient.

"Here." He handed her a cartridge.

She took it and worked once again to insert it into the gun. Calan waited until she finally maneuvered the cartridge inside.

"Good. Now put the magazine back into the gun."

Smiling her triumph, she did as he asked. "I'm not going to shoot anyone, you know."

He moved around to her backside. "The key to this is lining these two rear sights with the front sight." He guided her arm so she raised it. "You aim the front sight so that it's centered between the rear sights. And you adjust your aim if it's windy."

She angled her head to look up at him. "I adjust my aim?" She doubted she'd ever get good enough at this to have to remember that.

"I just want you to be able to hit someone before they hit you."

Put that way, she faced the trunk of a tree about a hundred feet away and made a gallant effort to aim well. She pulled the trigger and the pistol kicked back hard, forcing her hands up and making her bump into Calan.

"Good. Keep firing. Get a feel for how the pistol fires," he said. "That's why I wanted you to practice. You'll get used to it and it won't jerk you like that."

"Did I hit the tree?"

"No. You were off by about ten feet."

Ten feet?

"Shoot again."

She concentrated on the forward sight of the pistol and fired when she thought she had the tree lined up the way he'd instructed. The pistol kicked back again but she didn't lose her balance and this time she saw dirt displaced by her shot.

"Closer," he said.

She fired again. Bark flew off the tree trunk.

"Yes!" She fired until the magazine was empty, hitting the tree three more times.

"You're a natural. I'm impressed."

She turned to face him, warmed by his compliment but not having any illusions about her prowess with weapons. "I'm not going to miraculously turn into Wyatt Earp after an hour of this, you know."

He smiled. "Like I said, I just want you to be able to hit a body."

The idea of that didn't appeal to her much. "What if I can't? I mean, what if I can't shoot another person?" She couldn't handle seeing someone get shot. How could she expect to shoot anyone?

"If they're firing at you, you'll fire back, trust me."

More like she'd run away. But she didn't tell him that.

The way Sadie handled the Beretta convinced Calan that she was tougher than either of them thought. Or maybe that was just him. Alert and beautiful, she walked beside him toward a restaurant on Bulevardi Bajram Curri. They'd already gone to the government ministry building, but a woman had told them Murati was out for a late lunch at the Villa Fendy.

Calan opened the restaurant door for her and she preceded him inside. White tablecloths covered wood tables that matched the wood trim around windows and a glass-partitioned private dining room.

A woman with dark eyes and hair that was pulled tightly back into a clip watched them approach. "Two?"

"We're looking for someone," he told the hostess, who gave a half bow and extended her arm in invitation for them to pass.

Calan put his hand on Sadie's lower back and they

walked through the restaurant. He searched the tables and spotted Murati conversing with another man. Calan had only seen pictures of him, but he looked more clean-shaven in person.

He approached and stopped at the table, Sadie by his side. Murati looked up with his lunch companion and his brow went from inquiry to recognition. Unwelcomed recognition. Odie had sent him Calan's picture in case something went wrong.

"You should not have come here."

"You and I have something to discuss."

"I am in a meeting. It will have to wait."

Calan reached into his back pocket and took out his wallet, opening it to retrieve the business card. "No, I'm afraid this can't wait." He showed Murati the card.

His companion looked at it, too, but Calan knew he couldn't read it from where he sat.

Murati's eyes lifted. Calan patiently met his gaze. Then Murati turned to his companion.

"Will you excuse me for a few moments?"

"Certainly," the man said, shifting his curious gaze to Calan and then Sadie, lingering there.

Murati rose and, glaring at Calan, passed him and led him and Sadie to the front of the café. The hostess watched them questioningly as they left through the front door.

Outside, Murati turned to face Calan.

"What is the meaning of this?"

Calan held up the card. "Start talking."

"Who are you?"

Calan chuckled darkly. "Don't play games with me." He held the card in front of his face. "Who is this?"

Murati didn't respond. Telling him would probably guarantee his death.

"Who did you work with to arrange our flight here?"

"I cannot reveal that information to you. Now please go. If anyone sees you with me—"

Calan stepped closer. "I don't have much to lose by killing you. I think you know that."

The man's eyes flickered back and forth between Calan's.

"Just tell me who you worked with," Calan said. He had to get something from him. Some kind of lead.

"Arber Andoni."

"Did Andoni kill my pilot?"

Murati looked nervously from his left to his right, checking the sidewalk and the street. People walked to and fro but none took notice of them. "No. It was not him."

Calan lifted his eyebrows. "No? Was it this man?" He held the card up in front of Murati's face.

Murati's eyes grew fearful and he didn't answer.

"I'll take that as a yes."

Sadie slid her hand under his arm and rested her hand on his forearm, which let him know she didn't like this.

"You have no idea what you are doing."

"Then enlighten me."

"You have interfered where you should not. Our agreement would have gone as planned had you not done so. There is nothing I can do for you now. Our business is finished. Leave now, and never return."

"Under any other circumstances, I'd have to agree with you. But this is much different than I anticipated. Whoever is after me has ties from Albania to Montenegro."

"It goes much farther than that, my friend." It was a piece of information offered genuinely. The man wanted Calan to believe him. Believe, and get away.

"Tell me what I need to know. Then I'll consider leaving."

Murati contemplated him a moment and then relented.

"I do business with Arber Andoni. He is a good man. But he is close to Zhafa."

"I thought you didn't know Gjergj Zhafa."

"He is a dangerous man." Murati didn't acknowledge the charge. "Not one to cross. That is why I ask you again, Mr. Friese, to kindly leave. I have a family. Surely you understand."

Yes, he did understand. More than any man should. Which was why he couldn't leave. "Where can I find Andoni?"

Murati shook his head.

"Where does he live? You can at least tell me that much."

He shook his head again. "I cannot."

"If you don't tell me, I'll find out on my own. I have the resources to do it."

Sputtering something fervently in Albanian, Murati said, "Stupid man. Do you have a pen?"

Sadie dug into her handbag and produced one.

Murati took that and then the business card from Calan. He wrote something down on the card. Handing the card back to Calan, he said, "Do not go to him at his home. Do not frighten his wife and children. There is no need."

"What will I find at this address?" Calan put the card back into his wallet.

"He is attending a party tonight. The restaurant at this address was privately reserved. I can anonymously arrange for you to be invited so that it does not appear you are seeking him out." Murati told him the time and place of the benefit. "It is a formal affair. Black tie. I will register you as Calan Friese and a guest."

Since Zhafa already knew who he was, he didn't see any harm in using his own name. Nodding his appreciation, Calan turned to Sadie. "Let's go." He wouldn't get any more out of Murati anyway. He didn't want to force him, either. Call him soft. He knew too much about protecting his own not to be soft when it came to things like this.

"Mr. Friese," Murati called as Calan put his hand on Sadie's lower back to get her moving.

He turned his head toward the man.

"You did not hear of the dinner from me."

Again, Calan nodded. "No one will know we were here."

"Thank you," Sadie said to Murati, her innocence painfully obvious. She clearly didn't belong in Calan's company. Not in this situation.

When they were far enough away, he said, "Thank you?"

"I felt sorry for him. What if he turns up dead like all the others who've crossed your path?"

"He won't. Andoni needs him. Without him, he doesn't have government approval. He'd be shut down."

"Still. You scared him."

"Scared him. Murati is making a lot of money on bribes. Andoni is probably his biggest donator."

"And Zhafa?"

Murati wouldn't have told him about the benefit if he hadn't known Zhafa would be there. "Zhafa is something else."

"Yeah, and that's what worries me. He's going to recognize us."

"It'll be too public. He won't do anything there." Afterward was another matter.

"So we're just going to act like we belong there?"

"Yes."

"I don't think I can pretend about that."

"I'll help you. Don't worry."

She didn't seem convinced.

It was important that she not make them stand out in a crowd tonight.

Before flagging down a taxi, he slipped Sadie's hand in his and tugged her so that she turned and bumped against him, her hands landing on his chest. While she stared up at him with startled eyes, he slid his arm around her and pulled her closer.

"I won't let anything happen to you," he said.

Her transparent, sea-blue eyes remained wide and searching. Somehow he needed to find a way to take her mind off the danger. He did what came naturally.

Lifting his hand, he ran his fingers along her face to the back of her head, sinking his fingers into her soft hair. Her eyes half-mooned with desire and he was glad to see it was that easy. It fired a surge of answering response in him. Like a switch, she was back in his arms.

"Sadie," he murmured.

She tipped her head back a little and he heard her breathing through her parted lips. He pressed his to them.

A sound erupted from her and she wrapped her arms around his neck. He felt her feminine curves against him and ran his hand down to her ass.

He wished they were somewhere private. Raising his head, he looked down at her sultry face and the way her eyes drowned with his. He wanted her so much he ached. Good for both of them they didn't have time.

Chapter 8

Tension hung thick in the taxi as it rolled to a stop in front of an upscale Italian restaurant in the heart of downtown Tirana. More than once today, he'd almost taken Sadie back to the pension. Only the urgency in finding dress clothes had stopped him, that and the way Sadie had sulked the entire time. She wasn't happy with the way he'd shown her that nothing had changed between them.

He got out of the car and extended his hand to her.

She hesitated.

Being together disconcerted him, too. Seeing her in that dress after she'd come upstairs from the bathroom hadn't helped. By the time he finished taking in her long legs and those shapely hips and tasteful amount of cleavage exposed in that tightly fitted black dress, he'd caught her checking him out, too. The desire was always there, a beast that needed constant taming…or relief. And there was only one way to take care of that, the way they both needed to avoid.

He wasn't sure how much longer either of them could fight it. The night at the villa had teased them both with a taste. After kissing her today, the zapping energy between them might as well set the taxi on fire.

Was he confusing what he felt for her with phenomenal sex? It was that good with her, but how could he turn away from Kate like that? So easily.

At last, Sadie gave him her hand. When she stood, he didn't want to move. He just wanted to keep looking at her beautiful face, lightly made up with soft tendrils of hair falling around it from her artfully arranged updo.

"Remember, it's too public for Zhafa to do anything. We'll be fine as long as we're careful." Shutting the taxi door, he stepped onto the sidewalk with her.

"Public is good," she said.

Hearing her double meaning, he smiled and guided her to the entrance. He told the doorman they were there for Andoni's party. The doorman allowed them to pass.

Inside, a band played a jazzy tune. Chandeliers were set low to shed romantic light on the wide, open room of white-topped tables. Men in suits and women in varying styles and colors of cocktail dresses nearly filled all the tables. He'd deliberately made sure he and Sadie showed up fashionably late. Too early could be dangerous.

Scanning the room, he spotted Andoni. He sat at a table with a lovely dark-haired woman whose diamonds sparkled like strobe lights, and another couple.

A waiter appeared with a tray of champagne and said a word in Albanian that must have been, "Champagne?"

"Grazie." He took two glasses and handed Sadie one of them.

She took it and met his eyes as she sipped.

Seeing a table that would give him a good view of Andoni, he put his free hand on Sadie's lower back and guided her there, not missing virtually every man they passed turning to stare at her.

On a typical day, Sadie wasn't an extraordinary beauty, but the way she'd enhanced her features and displayed the enticing shape of her body highlighted her interesting good looks. She had her own brand of beauty, the kind that grew on a man so that he never got tired of looking at her. Nothing Barbie about her.

Waiting until she sat first, Calan sat beside her, facing Andoni. The man hadn't looked their way yet, and no one else seemed to notice them, either. That was good.

"Where is he?" Sadie asked.

"In front of the dance floor."

She looked toward the dance floor and the band. "The one with the woman in all the bling?"

"That's the one."

"Is the man sitting with them Zhafa?"

"I don't know." He watched a man from the table next to them get up and lean down to talk to Andoni's wife. He was an older man. Calan looked at everyone sitting at the table he'd vacated. Three men and one unhappy-looking woman.

"That man talking to them came from the big group over there," Sadie said.

Her observation unexpectedly impressed him. "Yeah, I noticed that, too."

"What are we going to do? Just watch?"

"After everything gets going we'll start mingling."

"You mean after everyone starts getting drunk?"

He chuckled. "Yes. You sure you don't want to come to work for TES?"

"TES?"

Realizing his mistake, he inwardly reprimanded himself. Being with her constantly must be wearing on him. Or was he getting so comfortable with her that he forgot to watch what he said?

"What does it stand for?"

"I shouldn't have told you that."

Her eyes blinked and radiated her appreciation. "But you did."

Yes, he had. And that disturbed him. It was too easy being with her.

"You might as well tell me now." She gazed at him beguilingly as she sipped her champagne.

He found her completely adorable, and she was right. "Tactical Executive Security." He hadn't given much away. She'd never find the name in any directory.

"How long have you been with them?"

"Six months."

He could tell by the sobering of her eyes that she understood the significance of the timing.

"Why TES?" she asked.

He'd gone to work for TES after his girlfriend had been killed. "They're business is counter-terrorism. They were going after Dharr and I wanted to be the one to catch him." He figured he didn't need to keep this from her anymore.

"So you joined them."

"Yes."

"Why? You were already chasing him."

"TES had the connections I needed, the resources. Equipment and money." And a cause he believed in. "With them, I could move a lot faster."

"And secretly."

"Some of our accomplishments do reach the news."

"But no one is able to tie them to TES."

"No." Not so far. "Most people would cheer us on."

"Except maybe our government, if your actions compromise international relationships."

"Nothing is compromised if the organization behind the mission is unknown."

He saw her consider that without any decisive favor for one side or the other. "Are you going to keep working for them?"

Dharr was dead. "Yes." His thirst for revenge had been satisfied but not his thirst to squash terrorism.

"You say that with such conviction."

Her dreamy expression told him she liked that. Maybe knowing he worked on the side of good—albeit in secret—made her feel better. He didn't know how to tell her she shouldn't be so enamored.

"What made you decide to join the Army?" she asked, sipping the last of her first glass of champagne.

He flagged a waiter over and got her another one. That made her smile with that same dreamy look in her eyes.

"I come from a long line of military men," he answered her question. "My father lost a leg on one deployment, but he never spoke one negative word against the military. He was a true patriot."

"And so you grew up with the same ideals?"

"Yes."

Her dreamy smile changed to curiosity. "You don't sound very happy about that."

"I've seen things that made me question the way our military operates. It made me wonder if some rules aren't in our best interest."

"Do you mean the attack in Yemen?"

He nodded. "One of our own took sides with terrorism. I caught Dharr, but I didn't do it by following rules or making sure I was politically correct. We'll never beat terrorism by following rules. Terrorists don't care about diplomacy. They don't follow rules. That makes catching them a dirty job."

"But you were a Delta soldier. Every mission you went on was secret."

"Yes, they were secret, but none of them gave me Dharr."

"In other words, the only way to win the war on terrorism is to throw morals out the window and kill without mercy."

That was exactly the way he'd killed Dharr. "You think terrorists deserve to be treated morally?"

"No, but the governments where they take refuge do."

"Not if they have their heads buried in the sand. At that point morality has very little to do with it. That's the beauty of working for a company like TES. We go in and take out our target before anyone knows we were there or who was there. The media don't know. Our government doesn't know, not technically anyway, and the government where our target is located doesn't know. If nobody knows, no one gets hurt except the one who deserves to be hurt."

Sadie sat back and sipped her second glass of champagne. He sipped his, too, and watched her think over what he said.

Finally she set her glass down and looked at him. "You have a lot of passion on the subject."

Yes, it was something he felt very strongly about. "I'm going to kill as many terrorists as I can until I'm physically unable to do it anymore."

Her eyes blinked slowly and he could swear he saw her attraction to him grow the more she heard what she called his passion.

"You have a really good reason for wanting to do that," she said.

He didn't want to talk about what had led him down this path, so he didn't say anything. Leaning back like her, he drank more champagne and checked the tables around

Andoni. The older man had gone back to his table. One of the men who'd sat there had gotten up and now stood with a group of others.

"Why didn't you tell me all this from the beginning?"

He turned to Sadie. "Would you have gone with me if you had known?"

"You have a just cause for doing what you do."

"Is that a yes?"

She didn't answer at first. "I don't know what I would have done."

Because her reasons for wanting to escape had more to do with her feelings than his background? Yes, and because of that he had to watch her.

Surveying the rest of the crowd, he saw there were more people here. Many had abandoned their tables to stand and talk near the two bars in the room or to dance. It was time to start mingling.

Just when he was going to ask Sadie to dance, a couple approached their table. Late arrivals.

The woman asked something in Albanian.

"Do you speak English?" Calan asked.

"Ah, Americans," she said in accented English. "We travel there a lot." She looked from him to Sadie and back again. "Are these seats taken?"

She wore a strapless white dress and held a small matching purse. Diamonds dangled from her ears and around her neck. She appeared to be in her late forties, with light green eyes that had probably been striking in her youth. They were her best feature—otherwise she wasn't all that attractive. The man with her looked pretty much like every other man in the room, except for his big nose and mouth. He was also about an inch shorter than his date. They weren't married, unless they both had chosen not to wear wedding rings.

"No," Sadie said before he could answer. "Would you like to join us?" She gave them a beaming smile.

Calan noticed how hard she tried to be friendly and wondered why she thought she had to.

"Why, thank you," the woman said, all sugary and false. "I am Edona and this is Pietro." She sat in the chair beside Sadie. Pietro sat next to her and to the left of Calan.

"I'm Sadie and this is Calan," Sadie said, still smiling in an overexaggerated way. "That's a lovely necklace you have on."

The woman all but gushed her pleasure. "Why, thank you."

Were they going to have to listen to her say, "Why, thank you" all night? Calan watched her eye Sadie like a jealous woman looking for flaws. She made no return comment on Sadie's appearance, which was about ninety-five percent higher on the knockout scale than hers.

"What brings you to Tirana?" Pietro asked.

"Just visiting," Calan said, looking over at Sadie, hoping she'd take his lead.

"Vacationing?"

"Yes. We came over from Italy."

The man nodded, taking a glass of champagne for his girlfriend and another for himself from a waiter who had approached with a tray.

"Are you from here?" Sadie asked, looking at Edona.

"Pietro is from Rome, but we live in Tirana." Edona lifted her head higher. "In a villa on the coast."

"We rented one in Montenegro." Sadie glanced over at Calan and he could tell she wondered if she was supposed to say that.

Her distraction made her miss the haughty narrowing of Edona's eyes. "We've been to Montenegro many times."

Sadie smiled. "I love to travel."

"What is it you do in America?" She looked from Calan to Sadie.

Enjoying the show, Calan relaxed back with his glass of champagne and waited for Sadie to answer. This ought to be good.

"We…I…my father runs a restaurant corporation and Calan is a business analyst."

Calan was momentarily awed by her quick thinking.

Edona's brow lifted. "Hmph." She looked at Calan and checked him out.

"What company are you with?" Pietro asked.

"Homeland Bank."

The other man nodded. "Big company. Do you travel a lot?"

"Yes. Mixing business with pleasure right now." He turned to Sadie and smiled.

"I know what that's like." Pietro chuckled, glancing over at his girlfriend.

Her superior expression re-emerged. "Pietro is a top executive for Andoni International Airport."

Calan filed that away for now. That's how he'd gotten his invitation to the party. He worked for Arber Andoni.

"What kind of restaurants does your father run?" Pietro asked Sadie. "What's the name of his company?"

Her face fell a little. She didn't want to talk about this. He didn't want to either, and would have stopped her if he wasn't sure Zhafa already knew who she was.

Edona didn't want her to, either, Calan saw.

"The Mancini Corporation. Table Mesa Kitchen. Pascoli's. Salt Reef Bar and Grill."

"I know of them. Your father is a very successful man."

Sadie's face remained unhappy. She glanced at Edona and saw the jealousy oozing off her. Except Calan doubted she recognized the other woman's jealousy. Maybe she only saw the animosity and assumed she wasn't fitting in again.

"What is it you do?"

Sadie turned to Pietro. "I…"

"Sadie's an artist," Calan said and felt her startled eyes find him. He smiled fondly at her, not having to act. "She oil paints."

Edona laughed. "Good thing your father makes a lot of money. You'd be starving otherwise. It's so hard to make it as an artist. It's the same with musicians and writers. So many don't make anything at all."

Sadie's face began to flush.

"Her paintings have sold," Calan informed the shallow woman.

Edona passed a glance over him and then returned her attention to Sadie. "Of course they have." She patted Sadie's hand. "I don't have to work, either."

"Edona's family runs a farm near Tirana," Pietro said.

Calan caught the alteration in her eyes and saw right through her. Her family didn't make much money. She only made people believe they did. What she really wanted was to have what Sadie had. The real thing. Lots of money. Someone to take care of her while she floated from one social event to the next.

"Oh, what kind of farm? Are there animals?" Sadie asked.

"No." Edona sounded annoyed. "We grow produce."

"Oh. My father gets a lot of his produce from a big corporation. They must have a lot more land than your family does. Because it's a corporation, not a family-run business. All I mean is, it's bigger…the corporation."

Despite Sadie's attempt to smooth her words, Edona almost visibly fumed with anger.

"You must have a very close-knit family," Sadie added.

Calan had to stifle a laugh. She tried so hard to make others like her that she ended up saying the wrong things. But the people who misconstrued what she'd said weren't worth the effort to begin with.

Edona bristled but said nothing. She took an aggressive sip of champagne and glowered at Sadie, who noticed and sort of shrank in her chair.

Calan turned to Pietro. It was time to start digging. "How long have you worked at the airport?"

"A little over a year."

Underneath the table, he reached over to Sadie's knee and put his hand there, caressing her bare skin with his thumb. Her head turned abruptly but she didn't resist him. Instead, he sensed she understood why he'd done it. He was certain when she put her hand over his and smiled.

"You like it?" Calan asked Pietro.

The man gave a noncommittal nod. "Pays good." Beside him, Edona gloated over at Sadie, who again noticed and met the woman's gaze with more confidence than before.

"How do you know Arber?" Pietro asked.

"I don't know him well."

Pietro frowned. "Then how did you get invited? This is Mr. Andoni's fortieth birthday celebration."

"We were invited through a common acquaintance. Because we didn't have any other plans, we thought we could use a nice night out." He gave Sadie a meaningful look, and she leaned closer to him with infatuation glowing on her face.

As he hoped, Pietro didn't press on who the common acquaintance was. But Edona glowered as she noticed the exchange between him and Sadie.

Calan decided to spare Sadie any more torture and said to the couple, "Will you excuse us?"

Standing, he extended his hand and Sadie took it. He led her to the dance floor and twirled her gently toward him, bringing her flush against him and holding her close.

"You did that on purpose," she said.

Partially true. "Can you blame me?"

She was still smiling warm and soft up at him, relaxed in his arms, moving with him to the music. There were several other couples dancing but there was plenty of room to move.

Calan saw that Arber had left his table and had joined the group of men he'd seen earlier. He started talking to a man standing next to the one who'd left the older man's table. His head tossed back for a loud laugh. Calan caught the man standing next to them looking right at him, and he didn't look pleased. In fact, he looked downright ticked. Zhafa. It had to be.

"Get ready for a confrontation," Calan said.

Sadie's glow dimmed and she began searching around the room. "Why? Has someone recognized us?" She looked up at him. "You said no one was going to shoot at us tonight."

"They won't. Not in here."

When her eyes grew more frightened, he said, "There are too many people here for anyone to do anything. Stop worrying."

"What about when we leave?"

"Stop worrying," he repeated, running his hand up her back and down again. He was beginning to really like her intelligent mind. When her eyes blinked in response to the caress and she softened again, he wondered if he'd forget the reason they were here and lost himself in her.

Bad idea.

"Let's go get some more champagne." He stopped dancing and took hold of her hand.

"We just got out here," she complained.

He led her to one of the waiters and handed her a fresh glass, then took one for himself.

She sipped and began looking around the room. Calan kept his eye on Zhafa, watching him look over at him and Sadie every once in a while.

"Who's that older man who keeps going over to Arber's wife?" Sadie asked.

He first turned to her, then followed her gaze to Arber's wife, who smiled at a tall, gray-haired man with a barrel torso and dark eyes. There was a close connection between them. They knew each other well.

"I bet he's her father," Sadie said.

Again, her observation impressed him. She was full of surprises. Rich socialite on the surface, but underneath…

The older man leaned down and kissed Arber's wife on her cheek and murmured what Calan assumed were terms of endearment. Then he walked away.

"Definitely her dad," Sadie said. "They look alike, too."

They did. "You sure you don't want to come to work for TES?" he teased.

And he got what he wanted—her unappreciative pout. Chuckling, he slipped his arm around her waist and pulled her closer to his side. Like on the dance floor, she melted against him.

Checking the group of men with Arber, he saw that they'd broken up. Arber had returned to his wife's side and he didn't know where Zhafa had gone.

"Arber waited until his wife's father left before he went over to her," Sadie said.

"How do you know?"

"I saw him looking over there when they were talking. I don't think he likes his father-in-law."

Calan watched Arber talking to his wife. She wasn't happy with whatever they were talking about.

"That's interesting," he said.

"Maybe you should try to find out her father's name," Sadie suggested like a true operative.

Calan chuckled and that brought her head around. When he saw her bewildered expression, he chuckled again.

"I don't understand why you think it's you who's lacking when you meet rich people," he said, trying not to fall harder for her than he already had.

"What do you mean?"

"You're an amazing woman, Sadie Mancini. Don't ever let anyone make you feel any less."

"What?"

"Do you think Edona would have noticed a conflict between Arber and his wife's father? She wouldn't have noticed the fact that he probably *is* her father. And I know she would have never thought we should find out his name."

She eyed him suspiciously. And then she rolled her eyes. "You know as well as I do that I'm not cut out for this kind of work."

He wasn't so sure about that. With a little practice she could be an asset to an intel team.

"You have balls showing up here," a heavily accented voice said in English.

Calan turned to his right, Sadie stepping along with him, to see the man who'd spoken with Arber.

"Gjergj Zhafa," Calan said. "I've been waiting to meet you."

Zhafa studied him and then glanced around the room. Calan wondered what he was looking for and hoped it wasn't his henchmen.

Sadie clutched to him, her arm slipping under his.

"I've heard a lot about you," Zhafa said.

"Then you know why I had to do what I had to do."

"Your business with Abu Dharr is your own."

"Was," Calan corrected.

"Yes, and although that has caused me some inconvenience, it has not impeded me. There is another matter that is very much my business."

"Are you working with one of Dharr's associates? Is his network that extensive? You might want to be careful who you choose as your friends once word of that gets around."

His meaning didn't go unnoticed by Zhafa. "You are no longer with the military."

"No." He'd expected his résumé to be passed around. "I'm independent now." He met Zhafa's dark, beady gaze dead-on and watched the man register that.

"One man against this organization is no concern of mine."

What did he mean by "this" organization? "I said I was independent. I didn't say I was self-employed."

Again, he watched Zhafa process the meaning behind the words. "You are good, Mr. Friese, but you are no match against me. You would be wise to reconsider what you are doing and return what is mine."

"If you weren't doing business with terrorists, I might be inclined to do as you ask. But since you are..."

"Then you've made up your mind." Once again his gaze passed over Sadie. "That is a shame."

The silent innuendo angered him beyond his control. "Be careful. I take threats like that to heart. Look at Dharr."

"Then give me back my money."

Calan said nothing. Instead, he looked toward Arber's table, who'd noticed him talking to Zhafa. Zhafa looked there, too, and then back at Calan. He smiled without humor. "It would seem we have nothing more to discuss."

"No need to be skeptical."

Zhafa's eyes narrowed at Calan's sarcasm. He gave Sadie a small bow. "Madam."

Sadie didn't acknowledge him with anything more than a wary look. Zhafa left and walked over to the table next to Arber's. Calan watched Arber look over at Zhafa and then directly at him and Sadie. There was no sign of recognition, just curiosity over who Zhafa had been talking to. But it would only be a matter of time before Zhafa spread the word.

Calan put his glass on a tray on one of several small tables. "Come on."

"Are we leaving?" Sadie put her glass on the table, too.

"In a minute." Taking her hand, he walked to one of the bars first and asked the bartender, "Who is that man over there, sitting at the table next to Arber Andoni? The big man with gray hair." Zhafa was talking to him now.

"Sorry sir, Mr. Andoni's wife arranged everything."

"That's Alek Dervishi," a man standing near the bar said, holding a drink. "Lulyeta Andoni's father."

Dervishi.

He knew the name. One of his friends who worked for the FBI had mentioned him. Calan tried to remember what he'd said.

"All the rumors are true, too," the man said, smiling knowingly.

That's when it hit him. Alek Dervishi was a well-known Albanian mobster. The FBI agent had said he had people all over the world, even in New York. Calan hadn't even considered the possibility a man like that was behind the meeting with Dharr. He hadn't been that big, or so Calan had thought. And the Albanian mafia hadn't shown up on TES's radar as an organization involved in terrorism.

Did Zhafa work for him? He must. No wonder they'd been spotted so easily. At the embassy. The airport. In Montenegro. Dervishi had people everywhere. And here in his homeland, everyone knew him.

"Thanks," he said to the man and then guided Sadie toward the exit.

He looked toward Dervishi. He'd gotten up from his seat, but Zhafa was still there, watching Calan and Sadie leave.

Outside, the doorman flagged them a taxi.

"You know him, don't you?"

Searching his surroundings, assured they wouldn't be followed, he climbed in the taxi and sat next to her, telling the driver to take them downtown. They'd get another taxi from there. He didn't want to risk being followed. And he also didn't want to worry Sadie any more than she already was.

"Who is Alek Dervishi?" she pressed.

He turned to look at her. This was going to get bad.

"Tell me."

She wasn't going to let up until he did. "Someone very powerful." He hesitated. "And dangerous."

"How do you know that? How do you know him?"

"It's hard not to know about a man like that. He's Albania's biggest mafia leader." One with a worldwide reputation.

"Mafia." Sadie's face paled. "Oh, my God. We're goners. Dead. Gone. Dead and gone."

"Now you know why I wanted you to stay with me."

"You didn't know who we were up against."

He liked that she was saying "we" now.

"Calan, Zhafa was right. You're only one man. You can't fight a group like that."

"I know."

"Then give them their money back."

"You think that's going to make this go away?"

"What else can we do?"

Calan didn't know, but he had the best counter-terror organization in the world backing him, and it was time to take advantage of that.

Chapter 9

Sitting on the bed next to Sadie, Calan put his cell phone on speaker. She hadn't said much after they'd gotten back to the pension, and this morning she wasn't any different. If he turned his back once on her, she'd bolt. He could feel it. Her tension. Her urgency.

Odie answered on the second ring. "Took you long enough."

"We had a date last night." He winked at Sadie.

She met the wink with a stone wall. He pretended not to notice.

"You're in deep doo-doo, Friese. Hang on. Let me get Cullen." She didn't even take his bait when he'd said they had a date.

"Who is Cullen?" Sadie asked.

"My new boss."

When that didn't crack her stone wall, he gave her hand a squeeze.

"I've got you on conference," Odie's voice announced through his phone. "Is Sadie with you?"

"Yes."

"Calan," Cullen said, joining the call.

"I take it you found out who Gjergj Zhafa works for," Calan said.

"Alek Dervishi. How did you know?"

"They had a date," Odie tossed in.

So she hadn't missed his comment. "We went to Arber Andoni's birthday party. Everyone was there."

"That could have been dangerous," Cullen said.

Sadie's eyes rolled up and met his with a silent I-told-you-so.

"It was too public." He looked right into her eyes.

"Dervishi's organization spans at least fifteen countries," Odie said. "They call themselves The Order. They're best known for their special kind of brutality. Gives a whole new meaning to the word branding."

"What do you mean?" Sadie asked. "What do they do?"

"You think the Godfather was bad, this guy is downright gruesome. And it isn't just the way he kills his enemies. He kills people he even *suspects* have crossed him. His signature method is disembowelment—while the victim is still living, of course. He actually has his men trained to kill that way. Couple that with the number of countries he's infiltrated, and you've got one scary dude on your hands."

Sadie turned horrified eyes to him. He gave her hand another squeeze.

"It's no wonder we missed him going in," Odie went on. "His daughter married a normal guy. Andoni isn't part of the organization, other than allowing them the use of his airport. Dervishi dotes on his daughter. It's probably the only reason why he didn't kill her for not marrying someone in his organization. That's what he did to his stepson, when he married an American porn star."

"No wonder his wife looked so unhappy," Sadie said.

And Calan figured out she was talking about the woman they'd seen sitting at Dervishi's table.

"Yeah, I'm sure she'd have left him a long time ago if she didn't know he'd have her executed."

When silence began to stretch, Sadie said. "Does this mean we can go home now? There's nothing Calan and I can do here." She turned to Calan. "Are you going to return the money?"

"Returning the money won't make a man like Dervishi go away," Odie said. "Taking it probably pissed him off. He'll want dead bodies."

Namely, his and Sadie's.

"But we can't—"

"Don't worry, Sadie," Odie cut her off. "We have a team on the way. You're going to be all right. We do this sort of thing every day."

"I want to go home."

"There is no such thing as home for a while," Odie said. "These people will swallow you whole if you let them."

The horrified look left Sadie's eyes and a certain resolve took its place. She thought this was a hopeless situation. She'd thought it was hopeless before, but any doubt she'd had over whether or not to stay with him was obliterated by what Odie had revealed.

"Who did you send?" he asked Odie.

"A couple of snipers, an explosives expert and an ex-spy."

He smiled. "That ought to cover it."

Sadie's brow lifted incredulously.

"They'll be in Bari, Italy, by morning. You need to

sail there to pick them up. Will you have any trouble with that?"

"No." They already had a yacht. "We'll be there tonight." And once they arrived in Italy, he'd have to keep a close eye on Sadie. The temptation to leave him might overwhelm her better judgment.

"Are you sure no one saw us?" Sadie strained her eyes as she searched the disappearing Albanian shoreline. She never wanted to come back to this place.

"Yes. How many times are you going to ask me that?" he said as he navigated the yacht from the flybridge.

She bit her lower lip. He'd been exceedingly compassionate with her ever since that teleconference with Odie and the mysterious man who was his boss. Of course, he'd picked up on her anxiety. She didn't know what frightened her more—staying with Calan and facing the wrath of an international mobster, or trying her luck in getting home and depending on her father to protect her. Even with the "team" they were picking up in Italy, it couldn't possibly be enough to fight against Dervishi's organization. She felt doomed whether she stayed or left.

And then there was the matter of how she felt about Calan.

"Why don't you try to get some rest?" Calan said. "We didn't get much sleep last night."

They'd been up late from the party and the call came before nine. But getting rest was the most ridiculous suggestion she'd ever heard. Rest. How could she rest? Upset, she looked toward the bow and the sea that stretched ahead of them. Calan must have noticed her mood because he put the boat on autopilot and left the flybridge. He walked down to her on the main deck and stopped.

"Go put on a suit, then. There's a hot tub aft on the main deck. You could use a good soak."

She looked up at the overcast sky. It was chilly today.

"I'll bring wine," he added.

That did sound good. And what else was she going to do, stuck on this boat with him?

"I don't want to get this wet." She lifted her T-shirt to reveal the gun she'd put in her jeans like he did with his.

He smiled but reached for the gun and slipped it free, his fingers brushing her belly. Flaring sparks enflamed sexual frustration that had been building over the past few days.

"You don't need this right now."

Wondering if he knew how that sounded, she struggled with how it aroused her.

"No one's going to burst onto the deck tonight. We weren't seen leaving the marina. We didn't even have to check in with customs. I was cleared when I arrived. There's no way anyone will know where we're going or that we left at all."

That wasn't what worried her now. Her eyes fell to his T-shirt-covered chest and lower to his jeans.

"Go get your suit on."

She raised her eyes. "What about you?"

"I'll get my suit, too."

She didn't look away and neither did he. Something sweet and sultry passed between them. He was having as much trouble as she was. And now maybe they'd reached their limit of resistance.

He put his hands on her shoulders and steered her around to face the salon door. Instead of listening to her better judgment, she started walking. He'd put all their things in the master suite, which bothered her and tantalized her at the same time. She went down the stairs with him on her heels. In the suite, she dug out the suit he'd insisted she purchase in Montenegro and went into the bathroom to change. When she emerged, Calan was already in his trunks.

His gaze roamed over her body and stirred already-frazzled desires. She left the room with him behind her, hearing him retrieve a bottle of wine and glasses from the bar before following her out onto the aft deck. Putting the wine and glasses down, he uncovered the tub and turned it on. Steam rolled up into the night air and the sound of bubbles relaxed her even more.

She stepped into the warm water and sat back, closing her eyes. Yes, this was what she needed.

Hearing the cork pop free of the bottle, she listened to Calan pour the wine, the sound joining the bubbles. Reluctantly, she opened her eyes in time to see him climb into the tub beside her with two glasses of wine. He handed her one.

"Thanks." She smiled a little up at him, a natural reaction. She appreciated this diversion and chose to ignore where it might lead.

"Don't mention it." Sitting next to her, he sipped his wine.

So did she, having no idea what to say next. The sea was calm under a cloudy sky. Perfect weather for a warm bath. With Calan…

She was tired of fighting how well everything clicked with him. From the moment they'd met he'd appealed to her on so many levels. The danger he'd put her in didn't appeal to her, but *he* did. Never in her wildest dreams had she thought a special ops man who worked for a clandestine company would become a love interest for her… He'd told her about TES. He'd also revealed his deep conviction over fighting terrorism. He hadn't meant to, but he had. He'd shared all of it with her.

She doubted he was any more prepared for this relationship than she was.

And he saw things about her. When Edona had subtly been shunning her, he'd defended her.

You're an amazing woman, Sadie Mancini. Don't let anyone make you feel any less.

"You're awfully quiet," he said.

She sipped her wine to delay a response. But then she decided to ask what she was dying to know.

"Why did you say I was an amazing woman?"

"Because it's the truth. You are amazing. What's even more amazing is you don't see that about yourself."

"I do," she said. "But no one else seems to."

"People like Edona are insecure. They live behind the money and titles of the men they're with. They're nothing impressive all by themselves. People like that only feel good about themselves when they have more material possessions than everyone else around them. Titles and money over heart and soul. If you want to find people you can call friends, stay away from women like her."

And men, Sadie thought, looking up at the stars. "Those are the kind of people my father likes." She spoke the realization aloud.

"You want the wrong people to like you."

Did her father want her to like the wrong people? "So I should look for people who don't have money?"

"Who cares if they have money or not? Stop categorizing. Look for heart and soul."

She did categorize. Adam had money and came from a similar background as her. Even Edona came from a similar background. She didn't have family money, but she didn't have to work. The men she'd dated who hadn't had money fooled her into thinking they did. Her problem was wanting anyone she thought her father would like to also like her.

She didn't take any time to find out what kind of person they were, when she should spend a few minutes doing exactly that. Then she could simply walk away and spare herself a lot of agony and self-defeating behaviors.

From now on, as soon as someone started making her feel the way Edona had, she'd know it wasn't right. That could be her gauge. But how could she recognize heart and soul?

Looking over at Calan, warmth enveloped her. He could be her gauge for that. Whether he realized it or not, they had that together.

Still holding on to her glass, she leaned closer to him. "Thank you."

He grinned. "You're welcome."

Ignoring the little voice warning her not to do anything to make her feel more for him than she already did, she kissed him. Moving back, she met his now-smoldering eyes. This felt too good to give up. She put her glass of wine on the edge of the hot tub and then took his and put it next to hers. He let her, watching her with those gorgeous eyes.

Riding the buoyancy of the water, she slid her hands over his wet chest and straddled him, feeling feather-light sitting on him in the water with all the warm bubbles gurgling.

"I said you're welcome."

She smiled and kissed his mouth again. "You're an amazing man."

He kissed her back, their mouths melding and igniting an undeniable flame.

She couldn't get away from this. He touched her and she was lost in magic. He was the man she'd met that first night in the hotel, looking out for her, caring about her. He was doing that now. Caring about her, about how she categorized. He could relate to her. No man had ever been that way with her.

His hands moved over her back, emerging from the bubbly water to hold her closer. One hand slid into her wet hair and he pressed her mouth harder to his. He angled his head and took a deep taste of her with his tongue.

She lost control of her breath. She was hot all over and the temperature of the water had nothing to do with it. Calan and all that he was did. Him. He was what made her want to celebrate like this, celebrate the love that was growing between them, even though he couldn't see it.

But what if he could?

Putting her hands on each side of his head, she gave all she had to the kiss, satisfied when she heard a sound rumble deep in his throat. He moved his hands to her butt and slid her higher up his lap, over his erection. It made her shiver and grind herself on him more.

Feeling his fingers work the clasp of her suit, she pulled back as he loosened the top and then untied the straps around her neck. He pulled it free and tossed it over the edge of the hot tub, his hand colliding with the wine glass nearest him. Both glasses tipped over and crashed to the deck.

Sadie laughed and he chuckled.

"For once it wasn't me," she said.

He slid his fingers into her hair and brought her head down for another kiss, no longer smiling. She moved over him again.

Breaking free of the kiss, Calan looked down at her breasts and cupped them in his hands. He leaned forward and took one in his mouth. She felt his tongue graze over her nipple and pressed her lips to the side of his eye. She ground herself on him once again.

Swearing, he abandoned her breast and tugged his trunks down his legs. She rose up to give him room. As his trunks followed her top, she pushed her bottoms down. He hooked them with his finger and she heard their sloppy landing on the main deck planks.

Slowly, she lowered onto him. He guided his erection under the water. It was erotic looking into his eyes while he entered. Erotic, and more. This felt so real. He surrounded her soul and she gave in to that feeling. Bubbles churned and rolled as he slid all the way into her, made all the more intense because it was him who shared this with her.

She kissed him with airy brushes of her tongue until he began thrusting with his hips. She let her weight work for her, putting her hands on his shoulders for leverage. He had his hands on her hips, moving her with the thrusts, finding that place deep inside her. She was already building and cried out his name an instant before he moaned with his own release.

Afterward, she relaxed against him, wondering if she'd made a mistake letting go as much as she had. He seemed conflicted with the same thoughts as he continued to hold her close.

The timer on the bubbles stopped.

Sadie leaned back and found his eyes. His were a reflection of her confusion, a jumble of intense infatuation and fear.

Without saying anything or waiting for him to, she climbed out of the tub on the opposite side from the broken wine glasses and wrapped a towel around her, aware of him doing the same.

He picked up their suits and she headed for the master bedroom. When she reached it, she turned to shut the door, but Calan was right behind her.

"What are you doing?"

"You don't think I'm sleeping alone after that, do you?"

It warmed her immeasurably.

Leaving the door open, he let his towel drop and headed for the shower. Sadie dropped hers and followed.

He already had the water running and she admired his ass as he stepped into the tub. She pulled the curtains closed as she stepped in behind him, watching him tip his head back under the spray, his eyes closed.

She took advantage of his preoccupation to take in his magnificent body. He grinned when he opened his eyes and caught her. Smiling, she took her turn under the water while he soaped up and shampooed his hair. His hands got her soapy as he touched her when they switched positions, he rinsing while she soaped her own body and washed her hair.

He waited for her to rinse. She could feel him looking at her. It made her smile again when she caught him. Turning off the water, they got out and dried.

Sadie toweled her hair and ran a brush through it. When she emerged from the bathroom, she saw Calan drawing the covers back on the bed. This felt so domesticated, like they'd done it night after night for a long time. A real couple. One who was comfortable together.

She passed him on the way to the bed, catching sight of him hanging free and growing longer and thicker. She met his eyes with a smile before crawling onto the bed. His hands on her hips stopped her from going farther. She looked over her shoulder at him, but his attention was on other regions of her body. He urged her to move back, so she did.

With her knees on the edge of the bed and him standing behind her, he slid inside, slick and hard. Her range of movement was limited so she let him do most of the work. She wanted to see him but she couldn't. She had only the sensation of him pushing back and forth. He began slowly, a smooth, consistent mating, but then she heard his harsher breaths and then he moved faster, pushing harder.

Sensation swept over Sadie. She closed her eyes and just felt, until her entire body was consumed in a shuddering release. She called out his name over and over.

"Yes." She heard his gruff voice and felt him pulsing.

The fiery moment cooled and Sadie wasn't sure she was comfortable with the animal way they'd just had sex. It was the same at the villa. Calan seemed to sense that because he slid out of her and lay on the bed, opening his arm to her.

She curled next to him, forgetting her worries and not allowing herself to think about what would happen after they reached the U.S. If they reached it…

Sadie woke to bright sunlight streaming through open blinds. The white comforter was rumpled and she was alone on the bed, her backside exposed. Rolling onto her back, she let memories float into her mind and bathe her heart with euphoria.

Sometime during the night he'd awakened her, rolling on top of her and pushing her legs apart while he entered her. He hadn't asked, he'd taken, and she'd eaten up his tender aggression. It hadn't felt merely physical. His urgency had reached her. The resulting orgasm was the strongest she'd ever had, coming apart while he looked into her eyes and made love to her. Made love. She could think of no other label for it.

Had she dreamed that? No. But the way they were together was almost incomprehensible. How was this happening to her? How was this man making her feel so much for him in such a short amount of time? She wanted to stay like this forever. She wanted to stay with Calan forever.

The lovely euphoria died away and despondence took its place. She couldn't have him forever. She couldn't have him beyond her time with him now. If they survived.

Was it all the adrenaline she'd endured lately? Maybe the need for release had been so great that she was confusing real feelings with a basic need for serenity. Either way, it wasn't smart for her to continue along this path.

Tossing the covers aside, she sat up. The cabin door was shut, but she heard voices coming from the main-deck salon. Calan's team must have arrived.

She wasn't in the mood to be around anyone. She'd rather be alone and sort out her feelings, which were getting too big for her after last night. Best if she left now, before Calan hurt her any more than he already had by making love with her like that. So gritty. And so many times.

Crawling off the bed, she stood and went to the window, where she saw a forest of sailboat masts and motor yachts. They'd reached the Bari Darsena Vecchia Marina.

Going to the door, she listened to the voices.

"Killing a man like Dervishi isn't going to make this go away," a man's voice she didn't recognize said.

"Not even if we made sure he got his money back," another man said.

"I agree," she heard Calan say. "We have to try another tactic. Find something on him. Reason with him that way."

"Yeah. Speak his language. You leave me alone, I'll leave you alone," the first man said. "We come to an understanding with him."

"Still might have to return the money," yet another man's voice said.

"Not if it's going to be used for terrorism," Calan said. He was emphatic. Of course he would be, with his past.

Sighing, Sadie left the door and went into the bathroom.

She took her time showering, dreading facing Calan if he didn't feel the same as her. How sweet it would be if they had real potential. But that's not what the future had in store for her. And it was time to do something about that. Stand up for herself. Take matters into her own hands.

After drying her hair, she dressed in jean shorts and a white sleeveless top that hung just past her waist. Leaving her face bare of makeup, she grabbed her sunglasses and went to the cabin door. There, she paused to prepare herself before leaving the room.

Emerging into the openness of the galley and salon, two men sat on the sofa and two more stood near Calan. One of the men on the sofa had a huge duffel bag on the coffee table and he was sifting through its contents as if itemizing them. He lifted a pair of handcuffs and showed them to the man beside him with a grin. The other man shook his head in light derision and then saw her.

The rest of them noticed her at the same time. The man on the sofa dropped the handcuffs into the bag and sat back against the sofa. All of them were big, two of them huge. She felt like she'd just walked onto the set of *Ocean's Thirteen*, with a young George Clooney and a hairy Andy Garcia sitting on the sofa, and a Matt Damon and a Brad Pitt standing by Calan. They were dressed like tourists in Hawaiian and solid pastel shirts and jeans. The only thing giving them away were their tactical boots. She didn't have to see them bare-chested to know they were all armed. And each had on an earpiece.

"Sadie," Calan greeted. The intimacy of his eyes didn't match his voice. He was trying to hide their relationship. All business.

It made her stiffen. She'd expected his withdrawal, but she couldn't stop the pain.

He gestured toward George Clooney on the sofa. "This

is Reed Marshal." He was George to her from now on. "Owen Rourke." She nodded her greeting to the one next to him. "Eamon Dunne." She shook Matt Damon's hand. "And Merrick Hamilton." She shook the Brad Pitt lookalike's hand.

"Nice to meet you," she said. "So, which one of you is the ex-spy?"

A momentary silence stretched.

"That would be Eamon," Calan said.

"Is that your real name?" she asked Eamon. It wasn't very common and had a hint of femininity to it, although the man was anything but feminine. He was a bigger version of Matt Damon and had facial features that made him seem more intense.

"My mother named me after her father, who was Irish."

His dark hair and green eyes held traces of his ancestry.

"Everyone calls me M."

"Just M?"

He left it at that and Sadie figured she better not push.

"I'll go get us ready to leave," George said.

A flash of panic hit Sadie. "Already? Aren't we going to stay awhile?" Too late, she realized how transparent she was.

Calan frowned at her as though he'd hoped he wasn't going to be right about her and she'd just proven him wrong.

"I'll help you." Merrick followed George out the double-glass doors leading to the aft deck and disappeared.

"I'll move the money to the other boat," M said, and only then did Sadie notice the big suitcase near the sliding glass door. M picked up the handle and dragged it on its wheels onto the aft deck. Owen followed him.

And now Sadie was alone with Calan.

"Like you, M knows what it's like to be at the wrong place at the wrong time."

There had to be a reason he was telling her this, and it didn't take her long to guess. "He's here because he wants to be here."

"Yes, but there was a time when that wasn't the case."

"Well, then we do have something in common. What happened to him?"

"That's not important. What's important is you accept your circumstances until it's safe to send you home."

She didn't want to argue about that anymore. "Why are you moving the money?"

"We can't take it with us."

"What are you going to do?" Now that he had a team…

"Convince Dervishi he's better off not picking a fight with us."

"You really think that's possible?" Was TES that influential?

"There are ways."

Maybe, but Sadie didn't like thinking about them. Sighing her frustration, she turned and left the salon. Outside, she gripped the foredeck rail, longing to be on land right now.

She spotted M on his way back and watched him climb aboard without so much as a nod of acknowledgment. She looked toward the dock again. M reappeared, this time with Calan, and the two began loosening the moorings. As soon as they finished, Calan looked up at the flybridge and gave a thumbs up to George. Moments later, the yacht began to move. Bari slipped into the distance along with her dwindling spirit.

* * *

"Get below deck."

Sadie looked up at M from where she reclined on one of the foredeck lounge chairs, not understanding why he'd said that. Demanded, more like. He'd been navigating the yacht for the past hour or so.

He looked down at her. "Now."

Hearing the sound of another boat approaching, she turned to see a yacht headed toward them.

"We've got company," M said.

Sadie wasn't sure if he was talking to her or the rest of the team through his covert radio, but she left the flybridge and went down to the main deck. The other yacht was drawing closer, and she could see several armed men aboard.

She wasn't one to swear, but she did now.

Just then, Calan grabbed her wrist and hauled her with him into the salon and back to the master suite. "Stay here."

He left and shut the door.

Sadie went to the window and looked out. She couldn't see the other yacht from here, but she did hear a volley of gunfire cracking the air.

"I am sure getting tired of this," she muttered and scanned the room for a weapon. Opening her travel bag, she dug around until her hands came against the cool metal of the gun Calan had taught her how to shoot. She pulled it out and stared at it. Could she really fire this thing at another person? Pulling the slide back to make sure the chamber was loaded, she was about to go back to the window when a huge explosion accompanied a violent lurch of the yacht.

Losing her footing, she dropped the gun as she fell. Thrown against the wall near the bathroom, it took her a second or two to orient herself. Sitting up against the wall while the yacht pitched, she looked around for the gun. It had slid into the bathroom. She crawled there and picked it up, using the vanity to pull herself to her feet.

Another explosion hurled her against the bathroom doorjamb. Pain shot through her arm and she cried out. The yacht began to pitch toward the stern. Hanging onto the doorjamb, Sadie let go and let gravity help her toward the room exit. There, she opened the door and stepped into the hall. A roaring sound grew louder as she approached the salon. Reaching the room, fighting the rocking angle of the boat, she peered down the stairs leading below deck and chills of fear froze her for a second. Water. Rushing water. A rapidly deepening river of seawater was flooding the boat.

Sinking it.

And fast. They didn't have much time.

Spinning around, she bumped into Calan. He had both their duffel bags slung over one shoulder. Taking hold of her arms, he glanced down at the gun and then back at her face.

"We're sinking," she said up into his face.

"I know. We have to get into the lifeboat."

"What?" Her bloodless face felt cold. She understood they had to get off the yacht, but… "They're shooting at us!"

"I know." He took hold of her arm and helped her toward the glass door. "They won't kill us. They want the money, remember?"

"Why sink the boat then? What if the money was on board?"

"They know we wouldn't be that stupid."

Yes, Calan had a *team* now, but still. "They don't need all of us to make one of us talk." She squinted beneath bright sunlight and craned her neck to see the other boat.

She caught a glimpse of several men on the main deck, holding automatic weapons.

Dread nearly overwhelmed her.

Calan tugged her in front of him and she stood against the starboard rail where there was a ladder. The others were already in the bright-yellow inflatable lifeboat. After Calan tossed their bags over, she stuffed her gun into the waist of her shorts. Climbing over the side, she stepped down the ladder, hanging on for dear life as the bow angled higher into the air. Jumping into the boat, she got out of the way as Calan followed.

Sitting on her butt, Sadie watched in horror as the yacht gradually disappeared beneath the surface, more and more of the bow being swallowed. The flybridge sank and then the last of the stern vanished. Now there was nothing between them and Zhafa's boat.

"Okay, we let them take us aboard and make our move then," Calan said.

"There's about ten men aboard," M said. "We can take them. Easy."

"Assuming they don't try to kill some of us off before we board," George said.

"Yeah, let's hope they aren't feeling cautious," Calan said.

Meaning they didn't know the men came from TES, much less that the organization even existed. They might assume the men who accompanied Calan and Sadie were crewmen on the yacht.

Sadie's heart drummed a hard beat as the boat maneuvered closer to the other vessel. At the stern, a man standing on the swim deck threw a line and Calan tied the lifeboat to the yacht. Three men stood on the main deck, aiming their weapons.

One of them said something in what Sadie guessed was Albanian.

"He's telling us to board," M said. "I'll go first."

"Sadie, you follow me," Calan said. "The rest of you stay close."

"I didn't know you spoke Albanian," George commented, sounding as if they were boarding a cruise ship instead of one commandeered by criminals.

"I can only decipher parts of it." M stepped onto the swim deck, holding his hands up.

"Follow me," Calan told her. And with a pounding pulse, she climbed on to the swim deck behind him.

George followed, Merrick and Owen next. The man on the swim deck said something to M, who climbed on to the main deck. The man waved the rest of them by with his gun.

Sadie crowded Calan, looping her arm with his. One of the three already on the main deck approached. Sadie cringed when he came to a stop in front of her. His breath smelled like cigarettes and booze.

"You. Come with me," he said in English.

Shards of fear sprayed her senses. She clutched Calan's arm with her other hand and inched closer, pressed against him now, his arm like a pole.

"She stays with me," Calan said.

The man raised his gun and pressed it to M's forehead. "She comes now or he dies. We only need you two."

Sadie lifted her gaze to Calan and saw the consternation in the low set of his eyebrows. He met her eyes.

"It's okay," he said to her.

What? "I'm not going with him!"

"It's okay," he repeated, and she realized what she'd thought was consternation was calculation instead.

The man grabbed her by the arm and roughly tugged

her. She reluctantly let go of Calan's arm, keeping hold of his gaze with hers. In his eyes she saw his promise and she drew strength and courage from it.

She looked at each and every one of his teammates and saw the same reassurance from them. These men were not afraid and their captors were underestimating them.

But that didn't mean things couldn't go wrong.

What would happen to her while she waited for them to act? What if they weren't able to reach her in time?

Her captor said something in Albanian to two others. When they fell into step behind him, she ascertained enough. She stumbled as the man hauled her toward the aft deck. She craned her neck to keep Calan in view. But he was busy talking to the other men holding them at gunpoint.

The man gripping her arm forced her into the salon of the yacht. This vessel was bigger and much more elegant than the one Calan had chartered. A huge red leather sectional with bright-blue pillows was accented by shiny brass lamps and picture frames. The ceiling was domed and had rings of brass trim. Sadie half expected the man to bring her before the sheik who owned it. Except it wasn't a sheik behind this. It was a mobster.

At the first door in a hall along the starboard side, he shoved her inside. But instead of closing the door and leaving her there, he came in behind her, and to her horror, two more men followed.

One of them was Zhafa.

Chapter 10

Watching Sadie being forced away almost made Calan do something he'd regret. Only M's hand on his arm stopped him, that and Merrick muttering, "Wait for it."

There were five men left on deck. Two had gone with Sadie, and there were two more in the pilot house. He hadn't seen Zhafa yet, but he was sure the man was on board. Dervishi would have sent him to finish his job.

The time would come when they could make their move. He'd wait but not much longer. Sadie didn't have time.

One of the five pressed his gun to Calan's head. "We go below. Now." He looked at each of Calan's teammates as if daring them with his fearless black eyes to try anything.

Calan turned. The remaining Albanians kept their guns aimed on his teammates. He looked into the pilot house. As soon as they passed they'd be out of sight. He glanced at M and saw that he'd noticed. Owen had, too. Merrick's gaze lifted to the pilot house and then he caught Owen's look, which Reed saw. They were all ready.

M and Calan were behind the others, M a little in front of him and to his left. An Albanian walked behind M to Calan's left. Merrick had gained the lead and was flanked by two Albanians. Owen and Reed walked side by side, with an Albanian behind them and in front of Calan.

About halfway to the aft deck, one of the leading Albanians poked Merrick with his gun and ordered him to stop. He then opened a door and gestured for Merrick to go inside. He did. Any second now the Albanians were in for a surprise. Feeling the gun still pressed to his head and the Albanian holding his shirt like a tether, Calan stayed in tune with the man's position. He didn't weigh what Calan weighed. In fact, all four of his teammates outweighed the Albanians.

They were out of sight from the pilot house. No one else was on deck. Merrick began to move, his arms going for the nearest Albanian.

Calan reached up and grabbed the barrel of the gun at his head and rammed his elbow into the man's sternum. That gave him time to turn and crush the man's throat with his hand. He fell before firing his gun, but another bullet shot harmlessly out to sea.

Owen, Reed and Merrick were fighting two Albanians. M was just finishing his second kill with a knife he'd retrieved from somewhere—probably his boot—stabbing the man through the heart. The other Albanian lay on the deck, his arm bent unnaturally and a clean slice on his throat. M must have finished with the fallen Albanian before the second could swing his aim around.

Owen knocked another man's gun from his hands and Reed shot him. Merrick finished choking the last one, his body the fifth to thud on the deck floor, partially lying inside the entrance.

"Owen, Reed, you take the pilot house," Calan said. There was no point in trying to be quiet. The gunshots must have alerted everyone by now.

Sadie backed up until her knees came against the bed. The cabin wasn't big, with only enough room for the bed and built-in cabinets and a desk with an attached swivel chair. Zhafa approached with slow, sure steps. He was satisfied that she was finally captured. She was his insurance policy. If she didn't tell him what he wanted to know, Calan would when he threatened him with her life.

Or so he thought.

The two other men who'd brought her to the cabin stood on both sides of the door. They were impeccably dressed, both in dark casual slacks and lighter-colored but plain, long-sleeved dress shirts.

She searched the hall beyond them. Where was Calan?

Zhafa came to a stop in front of her. Something told her not to let him see how frightened she was. She stuck her chin out and met his ugly brown eyes squarely. But when he reached with his hand and cupped her chin, holding her head there, she couldn't breathe for a second. An eerie smile curved his pale, dry lips, creasing skin that was mottled with age and poor health.

"Where is my money?" he asked in accented English. "I know that your boyfriend would not have taken it with him aboard his yacht."

If she told him, he'd kill her and if she didn't, he'd hurt her until she did. Neither consequence was to her advantage, so she didn't respond, glancing toward the door again.

"He will not come for you," Zhafa said.

"I don't know where it is." It was pretty much the truth.

It was at the Bari marina on a boat, but she didn't know which one.

Moving his hand from her chin to the back of her head, he took a handful of her hair and pulled, bending down so that his face was inches above hers. "I will kill each and every one of those men until you tell me what I need to know, and when only Calan is left, I will make him watch me slowly kill you. You can save them all if you tell me where my money is."

She spat at his face. "Liar."

Letting go of her hair, he straightened, wiping his face with the sleeve of his dress shirt. With his right hand, he slapped her. The force of it jolted her head and sent her falling. She landed on her hands and knees.

"Nail her to the headboard," Zhafa demanded.

Sadie crawled away. No one had checked her for weapons. Now she reached under her shirt and took out the pistol, rolling onto her rear and aiming it up at Zhafa.

The two men who'd left their stations at the door to come toward her stopped short.

"Nail yourself to the headboard," she retorted.

The sound of gunfire made them all look toward the door. But Sadie didn't keep her attention off Zhafa long. He faced her again and she saw his uncertainty. Who had fired the weapons and who would be left standing? She also saw him contemplating whether to make a move on her, overpower her and take control of her gun.

A moment later, Calan appeared through the doorway, followed by M and Merrick, who each targeted the two Albanians while Calan moved farther into the room, seeing Sadie on the floor and taking a few seconds to absorb the fact that she'd somehow obtained the upper hand.

"Drop your weapons," M said.

The two other men looked at Zhafa, who nodded once.

He didn't want to be shot, and he must know Calan would shoot him. The men dropped their weapons.

Calan moved closer to Zhafa and searched him for a weapon. He found none and stepped back.

Zhafa's deadly gaze stayed on Calan. "Who do you think you are?"

"Sadie." Calan extended his hand, the one not holding a gun.

She took it and he helped her to her feet. His eyes went down to the gun and back up to her face, where he carefully perused her. Lifting his hand, he touched where Zhafa had slapped her and then his eyes met hers. Emotion that had driven him to find and kill Dharr surfaced.

Turning, Calan moved close to Zhafa. He trailed the barrel of his pistol down the man's face and then pushed it into the soft flesh under his chin. "I should kill you for that."

"Why do you not?"

"I want you to deliver a message for me."

Zhafa grunted derisively. "A message for whom?"

"Alek Dervishi."

At the mention of the mob leader's name, Zhafa considered Calan. "Do you think he will care what you have to say?"

"He should."

Zhafa chuckled. "What is this message?"

"Ask him why he thinks I let you live."

"That is all? That is your message?" Zhafa chuckled. "You might as well kill me."

"Just tell him."

"Do you think you can negotiate with a man like him? Make him see reason? A man like Alek makes his own reasons. He will not listen to the reasoning of others."

Zhafa paused. "Perhaps you do not know him as well as you think."

"Perhaps he doesn't know me as well as he thinks."

Again, Zhafa considered him. "You are an arrogant man."

Sadie almost agreed. How did he think he could take on a man like that? She glanced at each of his teammates. None appeared worried about what lay ahead. They must have some kind of plan. One that had to work. Because if it didn't, these people would never stop coming after them. Or him, anyway. She wasn't so sure that once she was away from him she'd be in any more danger. His past experience had more to do with his motives for keeping her with him.

"Let's go," Calan said.

M planted his hand on the back of one of the men below his neck. "Move."

Merrick forced the man under his control out the door behind him and Calan followed with Zhafa ahead of him, glancing back at her to make sure she was behind him. On the main deck, Owen and George finished rolling the last of the bodies overboard. Sadie had to turn her head away from the gory sight.

She watched Calan and the others force Zhafa and his men into the lifeboat and untie it from the yacht. They drifted apart.

George and Merrick went into the pilot house and got on the radio, and Sadie didn't have to guess they were reporting missing men.

Stepping out of the dinghy after leaving the yacht anchored offshore, Sadie followed Calan onto the beach, unable to stop staring at the villa ahead. It wasn't a mansion, but it was beautiful in a charming, picturesque way. It looked newly constructed and all the landscaping was young and bursting with color and texture. Flowering vines climbed the white stone exterior, accented by black window trim and a cut-up red tile roof. There was a turret in the center with half-circle, tiered balconies on the second and third floors and a concrete patio that matched the shape, extending out into green paradise that opened to sand.

Yet again, she was struck with the contrast between the beauty surrounding her and their dangerous situation. If she wasn't so busy running for her life, this would be an ideal accommodation for some R & R. With Calan…

Her mind finished the thought. And then her mood fell lower than it already was. Last night was magical and she didn't want it to be magical. Magical meant she liked him and the way he made her feel far too much. It also gave her false expectations. But knowing that didn't stop her from thinking about him, how perfect they were together, how perfect last night had been. She wanted more. She didn't want it to end. But it would.

Searching the coast, trudging her way toward the villa, Sadie wished there was a way to get back to Tirana without Calan. They weren't far from Durres. If she could find a car…

Calan's hand on her lower back gave her a jolt. She looked up and over at him and saw his assessing eyes. He knew what she was thinking, but did he know it was him she wanted to escape? The threat of Dervishi was beginning to matter less and less.

Around the side of the villa, she followed M and Merrick along a tree-shaded stone path to the front. Calan and the others were behind her. A car passed on a badly maintained road and another was parked in the rock driveway of a villa across from this one. She couldn't see the villa to the south and the one to the north looked vacant. There were no garages and she saw no car parked there.

Merrick opened the door. He'd gone to the office of this rental complex to check in before the rest of them had left the yacht. Sadie walked inside, feeling trapped in a paradise that wasn't paradise at all. The villa, once again, was fantastic. Less modern than the one where she and Calan stayed in Montenegro but bigger.

She stopped and watched the five men move about, and Calan took both their bags to a room up an open stairway. It was a loft. Merrick and M disappeared down the only visible hall, and Owen and George tossed their things in the middle of the living room floor. Owen rummaged through the bag she'd seen him with before.

Sadie looked up at the wood railing outlining the loft and two things struck her. A, she didn't have to worry about things getting out of hand with Calan tonight, and B, it was going to be next to impossible to sneak her way out of here.

She had to think of something.

Calan reappeared at the top of the stairs and took them three at a time. His eyes met hers and stayed, assessing and exuding frustration. He joined George and Owen at the dining room table. Was he put off because he knew she didn't want to be here anymore? Was he taking it more personally than she thought?

She moved to the back of the couch, putting her hand there. M and Merrick passed her and went to the table where the others stood. Owen had spread out some papers on the table and was talking low to Calan, George listening. The three made room for M and Merrick.

Folding her arms, she leaned her hip against the couch and let out a heavy breath. Was she witnessing the team in action here? Were they talking low because they didn't want her to hear? Trying to be nonchalant while they discussed what lay ahead?

Arms down at her sides again, she went to the table and shimmied her way between M and Merrick, ignoring their looks along with the abrupt and lingering silence that followed. She was too transfixed by the images on the table. They were high-resolution satellite images. She bent down for a closer look. It was a huge mansion with all kinds of outbuildings. Each image appeared the same, but color and clarity varied. Some had clouds, and others didn't.

"What are the dates of these?" she asked.

When no one answered, she straightened and looked from one man to the next until she ended with Calan. She raised one of her eyebrows at him and cocked her head, hoping this was a good rendition of you-better-tell-me-now-or-else.

"Dervishi's compound," he said.

And she had to smile. "That's not what I asked."

"Yeah, but you would have."

"These look like they were taken at really different times."

She looked from each of the five men when, again, no one responded right away, pausing on M, who had a shrewd glimmer to his eyes. He seemed to like the fact that she'd noticed such a thing.

"They were," Calan said. "We got all the images we could find so we could study any changes."

"And find a way in," M said. "Or more appropriately, a way out."

She turned to M. "What are you going to do? Crash through his security gates?"

"No," M replied calmly. "We're going to be allowed access through those gates, and then we're going to negotiate with Dervishi."

Sadie looked incredulously at Calan. No wonder they were looking for escape routes.

"Cullen got us something on Dervishi that gives us plenty of leverage," he said.

"When did he do that?"

"While we sailed here. He has a really good hacker."

She looked pointedly at each and every one of them. "What did he find?"

Owen glanced at Merrick, who glanced at M, who turned unchanging eyes to Calan.

Sadie folded her arms again and looked at Calan.

He sighed and shifted weight from one foot to the other with a jerky movement that conveyed his frustration. "We have email transfers between several of his men, including Zhafa, that reveal traceable connections to Dharr and his organization, which is about to undergo some changes since his death. Dervishi's involvement won't look good to the rest of the world. He won't want to attract that kind of attention."

All she could do was stare at him. "Wow," she finally said. "I didn't even notice when all that happened."

"M took the call," he said.

She looked at M, who rewarded her with his usual and customary desensitized gaze.

"And if you're wrong?"

"That's what this is for," Calan indicated the images. "Contingency."

In case they needed to escape. In case something went wrong. Which, Sadie was almost a hundred percent sure, something would. What if Dervishi wasn't threatened by the emails? It might not be enough to worry him.

"Where will I be when you go to meet him?"

"In the car." Calan moved away from the table and came

to stand in front of her. "Where you'll *stay* until we're finished."

"What car?"

"The one Owen is going to pick up as soon as we're finished here," he said, eyeing her pointedly.

So that option was out. He'd be expecting her to try to drive away from him. He'd be watching her.

But maybe she could use that to her advantage.

Chapter 11

Calan's even breathing didn't reassure her. Wondering if he was really asleep, Sadie quietly slipped out from under the covers and got up. She needed to keep it to only him who came after her and not the other four, at least not until she had a chance to get a head start.

She went into the bathroom, shut the door and dressed, having purposefully left all her things in there. While she'd gotten ready for bed last night, she'd taken money from Calan's bag and put it in hers. Carrying the duffel bag, she walked quiet as a cat to the stairs, glancing at Calan, who still slept, or pretended to sleep. Tiptoeing down the stairs, she heard snores from the couch. Owen. George was on the floor.

On the main level, she searched through the darkness for Owen's duffel bag. Seeing it along the end of the couch, right under his head, she inwardly cringed. Of course, it'd have to be right there. But the sounds of his snoring bolstered her courage. That and the fact that the bag was open.

Slowly approaching, she looked behind her and up toward the loft. No sign of Calan yet. Crouching, she reached into the bag and felt around. Lifting a knife in a holster with a thigh strap, she put that in her bag and stuck her hand in the duffel again, this time pulling out the handcuffs. Checking on Owen as she stood, seeing he hadn't stirred, she went to the table where Owen had left the car rental keys. She already had the yacht keys. With another glance behind her, she headed for the front door.

Stepping outside, she closed it, caught sight of Calan coming down the stairs from the loft. Just as she'd expected. Closing the door, she ran to the rental where it was parked in the half-circle driveway in front of the villa. Locking one half of the cuffs to the handle, she pretended to bend over as if opening the car door.

Calan came around the rear and slid his arm around her waist. "Did you really think I wouldn't notice?" he asked with his face beside hers.

She snapped the other half of the cuffs to his wrist and twisted out from between him and the car, stepping back.

He looked from her to the cuffs and tugged his wrist, his face storming into an angry scowl. "Unlock these."

"I can't stay with you anymore."

That confession along with the adamancy of her tone softened his anger. The truth had become clear to him. The danger no longer mattered. What was happening between them affected her emotions too much. She was falling for him and didn't trust that he felt the same or would allow anything to progress beyond what they had here.

"Sadie. Don't," he said.

"I'm sorry." There was more she could say, more that her

heart needed to say, but she didn't have time. She turned and ran for the side of the villa.

"Sadie!"

She reached the slope and had to slow to watch her footing. Calan began yelling for the others. Her feet sank into the sand and she ran as fast as she could, whipping her head back for a quick look. No one was in sight. At the shore, she pushed the dinghy into the water. Jumping in, she worked to start the engine between glances toward the villa. Giving the engine fuel, she propelled the boat to its top speed. When she reached the yacht, she spotted shadows moving on the beach.

She slowed the dinghy and brought it alongside the yacht, tossing her duffel bag onto the swim deck and hurrying aboard. Starting the crane to lift the dinghy aboard, Sadie grabbed her bag and ran to the pilot house. On her way, she paused to check the shore. Four men stood on the beach and Calan was in the water. He was going to swim after her.

Lifting the anchor, she secured the dinghy and then hurried back to the pilot house, where she started the yacht engine. Pushing the throttle forward into a turn, she steered the yacht toward Durres. Glancing toward shore, she could barely make out the shape of Calan swimming toward her. He'd never catch her.

They would expect her to go to the marina, so she wouldn't go there. She'd get close enough so that she could walk to find transport to Tirana. She checked the GPS monitor to see where she was and where she was going and then set the Garmin system. There weren't any reliable weather updates she could access in Albania, but she wasn't going to venture far from land. And she had to make sure she stayed within the mapped channel surveyed to be clear of mines left over from Albania's communist past. Once she was satisfied with her course, she set the autopilot.

Going to her duffel bag, she strapped the knife to her thigh and then pulled the slide back on the pistol to make sure it was ready to fire. Not that she would have to fire it. The only way she'd need a weapon was if someone other than police or Calan got too close to her.

Now all she had to do was wait. More than Calan expecting her to go to Durres made doing so a bad idea. This yacht was stolen. Port authorities would want to see documentation like owner registration and insurance papers and her passport. None of that would jive. Leaving was easier than arriving in this country. She'd have to find a safe place to anchor and remain out of sight of the marina and then dinghy to shore and hope for some luck to go her way for a change.

It seemed to take forever to reach the area she'd chosen to anchor. Seeing the spit of land that jutted out just as the map displays indicated, she shut off the yacht lights and cut the engine. When it was safe, she dropped anchor, hoping the map of surveyed water was correct and there weren't any mines lurking. When nothing happened, she worked on lowering the dinghy. The shore was dark except for lights coming from some buildings to the south. When the dinghy was in the water, she climbed in.

She'd have to watch out for port authority officials. They watched the coast very closely. But even if she was caught, maybe all she had to do was tell the truth and ask to be taken to the embassy or the nearest police station. She'd rather get to the embassy herself, though. This wasn't a popular tourist spot and not the safest one, either.

Motoring to shore, she strained her eyes in the darkness and searched the beach. Nothing moved and no sounds alerted her over those of the waves washing ashore. There was a rocky incline beyond the sandy beach. She'd have to climb that and see which way to go.

Slinging her duffel over her shoulder, she found a path and climbed the slope. At the top, she stayed low and searched for anything that might be a threat. Still nothing.

Just then she heard the sound of a motorboat and looked back to see the port authority circling the yacht. Once they saw her dinghy, they'd come check it out.

She ran across a rocky, shrubby field. Reaching a road, she checked her surroundings again. There were houses to the south. One was dark and closest to her. The road to the north was dark, but that was the way to the marina and Durres. She'd have a hard time finding transportation away from the marina at this hour.

Headlights made her heart skip frantically. She faced the dark building and ran for it, going to the back and pressing herself against the wall, looking around the corner to watch the approaching vehicle.

It stopped along the road. Two men got out. They were talking but she couldn't understand them. She didn't think the driver had taken the keys. They walked toward the beach unhurried, suggesting they weren't expecting to find foul play, only doing a routine check. When they disappeared from sight, Sadie sprinted to the car. It was a faded tan Mercedes sedan.

Testing the handle of the driver's door, she yanked it open when she discovered it was unlocked. The keys were in the ignition.

Climbing in, she started the engine and turned the car around, pressing on the gas to race down the road. She felt lightheaded and her whole body trembled. She'd never done anything so crazy in her life! What if she was caught?

"Damn her!" Calan roared.

M glanced over at him from the driver's seat. He'd

insisted on driving, saying that Calan was in no shape to keep a low profile.

"She'll go the U.S. embassy," Merrick said from the backseat. He, Owen, and Reed were all packed in like sardines, their bodies too big for the mid-size sedan.

"She won't make it that far." Calan was sick with foreboding. He couldn't imagine Sadie on her own out there. And he hated how helpless that made him feel.

"I think she might surprise you," M said.

Reed chuckled from the backseat.

"They usually do," Owen said. "You're talking about a woman who thought ahead enough to take my handcuffs."

"And the keys to the rental car," Merrick said.

They'd had to hot wire it to start it.

"How did she know you had handcuffs?" Reed asked Owen.

Calan glanced back unappreciatively at the three. He wasn't happy about how easily she'd duped him.

"She saw him fondling them," M said with a note of derision.

Owen smirked at M through the rearview mirror, which he had a good view of sitting in the middle. "You never know when you're going to need them."

Merrick grunted.

"It's not the way you think," Owen tried to defend himself.

"We've seen your magazines," Reed said.

"Hey. I'm a man. You can't tell me you haven't thought of that. Or bought magazines."

"I prefer the real thing," Merrick said.

"Why do you think Owen has handcuffs?" M teased. The real thing…

"You guys are just jealous," Owen said.

Merrick turned to him. "I thought you had them in case you needed to bind a bad guy."

"That, too."

"How many women do you meet who like handcuffs?" Reed asked.

"He's never met one who has," Merrick said.

"How would you know?" M asked.

Calan was getting tired of their casual banter. Weren't they worried about Sadie?

Not like he was. In just a week she'd grown to mean more to him than he ever should have allowed.

"We weren't talking about me," Owen countered. "We were talking about Sadie. How many women do you know who'd outsmart one of us?"

Calan looked back at him. "She didn't outsmart me."

"She handcuffed you to a car."

Beside him, M chuckled.

"I didn't expect her to do that. I also didn't know she could navigate a yacht."

"She's the daughter of a wealthy restaurateur."

Yes, she'd spent a lot of time on yachts. He knew that. But Sadie was…Sadie.

Calan caught himself then. Sadie was Sadie. Helpless, socialite Sadie. Except that wasn't who she was at all. She was strong and intelligent. She was the Sadie he was getting to know. And he was no different than anyone else she'd met who'd turned their back on her. Not intentionally, but losing a wife and another woman he loved to the same evil man had taken its toll. Up until now, he wasn't sure he could give any woman what she needed. He'd thought it wasn't fair to Sadie for him to enter into a relationship in that condition. But that's exactly what had happened. A relationship had begun.

The degree of their intimacy, the urgency of it, the love

that stirred and had sprouted—was still sprouting—meant something. He felt something for her, something real, something powerful, a deep connection that wasn't going to break. Now that he understood, he wanted to spend more time with her. He wanted to have a relationship with her.

He wished she was here so he could tell her. But she wasn't. She was off on her own, trying to escape him, trying to go home, believing he'd abandon her as soon as this was over.

He didn't blame her for running. Had he been in her shoes, he'd have done the same.

A man waving his hands in the middle of the road jolted his attention elsewhere. Another man stood on the side of the road talking on a cell phone.

"Look over there," Reed said. "It's the yacht."

Calan barely made out the white shape of the boat just offshore and over the horizon of the slope that dropped to the sea. He couldn't see the shore, but he'd bet a dinghy was there.

"Keep driving," he told M.

"I wasn't going to stop," he answered, passing the men.

Calan looked back at the man now throwing a punch in the air at them, his mouth moving with angry words.

"At least we know she got away from them," Merrick said.

And Calan faced forward. "I guess I did underestimate her."

But that didn't mean she'd be as lucky if Dervishi ever caught up to her.

The sun had risen by the time Sadie parked on the side of the gas station where Calan had gotten gas the day he'd driven her to the embassy, more of a kiosk with a single attendant. Removing the knife from her thigh and the gun from her duffel bag, glad she hadn't had to use them, she got out of the car. She'd hardly be able to get past security in the embassy packing a big knife and a stolen gun. She looked around to make sure no one noticed her. There were no cars at the station and no window on this side of the kiosk. She hauled her duffel bag over her shoulder and walked behind the kiosk and then toward the street.

Glancing behind her as much as she dared without looking conspicuous, she walked the few blocks to the embassy. Cars drove by on the busy street, and she walked past other pedestrians who were slower on the sidewalk. She didn't see anyone who recognized her.

At the embassy gates, she approached the guard shack. An official approached her.

"I'm a U.S. citizen," she said. "I lost my passport and I'm here to pick up the replacement." She took in the gun at his hip and the automatic rifle he had over his shoulder.

The man studied her, then nodded and let her pass. She opened the door and waited for the man in front of her to finish his business. When it was her turn, she asked to see the duty officer who helped her get a replacement passport.

"Your name?"

"Sadie Mancini."

The woman picked up her phone. "There is a Sadie Mancini here to see you." After a moment she hung up. "He'll be right here."

Did that mean her passport was ready? Sadie smiled, unable to keep her elation from giving it an especially beaming quality.

The duty officer appeared with a smile. "I tried to call you at your hotel, but they said you checked out."

"Is my passport ready?"

"Yes, yes. Come with me."

Elation swam inside her as she followed him down a hall. At an office door, he stopped and let her in before him. She went in and turned.

"I will be right back. Have a seat."

Sadie sat in one of the two chairs angled before a cluttered desk and looked back at him.

"Can I get you anything? Water?" he asked.

"No. No, thank you." Just her passport. Thank God. She could actually leave this awful place legally and never return.

Leaving.

That meant never seeing Calan again. Barely aware of the duty officer closing the office door, she stared at the barred window and felt her heart sink for the first time since her escape.

Escape.

She couldn't really call it that. She didn't want to escape Calan. But he'd want to escape her as soon as they were in the U.S. and she couldn't bear that.

She'd have these memories that she'd lived with him and that's all. Meeting him. Sleeping with him that first time and again on the yacht. The yacht would stay with her the most. It's what had compelled her to do what she'd done. Trick Calan. Cuff him to the car door. Sail a stolen yacht close to Durres and evade port officials.

Really?

Had she actually done all that?

By herself?

Let's not forget she'd also stolen a car belonging to said port officials. Who was she? This was a side of herself she'd never gotten acquainted with before now. Most people she met saw her as a sheltered rich girl—not adventurous or brave or courageous. Incapable of taking care of herself, particularly in a life and death situation. She was a socialite whose biggest concern was what party she was attending and what she was going to wear...or in her case, which people she was going to try to befriend. Independent and resourceful were not words anyone would attach to her. But this other side of her had always been there. She'd always sensed it, always known she was capable of taking care of herself, but she'd gotten lost along the way, not knowing how to please her father and doing a bad job of trying. Now she realized she should have followed her heart. Her father may not have liked her choices, but she'd have found more success than she had forsaking her own needs.

Standing, Sadie went to the window and peered through the bars at the front of the embassy. Activity was moderate. Not busy today. She looked back at the door. It sure was taking a long time. She'd been in here for more than fifteen minutes now.

Looking at the bars again, a bad feeling filtered through her awareness. It wasn't significant that embassy windows would be barred, but they made her recall the officer closing the office door when he left. Why had he done that? Pivoting, she walked to the door and tried to knob.

It was unlocked.

Breath sighed out of her. She pressed her head against the door, calming her nerves. Then she lifted her head. She and Calan had been seen at the embassy before. What if someone had approached the duty officer? Bribed him, or threatened him.

Backing up, she searched the office. Lamp. Books. She went to the desk and opened drawers. Pens. She took a pen and held it so the point stuck out past her curled pinky finger.

The door opened and the duty officer entered with a smile.

Maybe she was overreacting.

"Sorry that took so long." He left the door open and extended a passport to her.

Relief came with a rush of elation. "Thank you." Taking the passport, she lifted her duffel bag. Everything was going to be all right now.

"I've arranged a taxi for you."

"I can't thank you enough." She was finally going home.

He let her leave the office before him and she hurried to the front entrance. Outside, an unmarked taxi waited. Glancing back, she didn't see the duty officer, but the taxi driver had gotten out and smiled as he opened the back door for her.

"Airport?" he queried in barely understandable English.

"Yes. Tirana International." She got in and he shut the door.

The driver went to the front and Sadie watched as they left the embassy. She didn't see anything suspicious outside the gates and, as they headed down the street, she began to relax.

She wasn't exactly sure where the airport was. They were close to the stadium and the hotel where she and Calan had stayed.

When the driver turned onto a side street, she knew something was wrong.

"Where are you going?"

The driver's eyes shifted to look into the rearview mirror, but he said nothing.

Oh, no.

Someone had gotten to the duty officer. The driver of this car worked for Dervishi. Fear clouded her thoughts.

Now what? She looked at the door. Should she open it and jump out?

The driver sped up and then sent her jerking forward as he turned another corner. Now they were in a weed-infested parking lot and approaching a badly deteriorating building that looked like a warehouse. Two cars were parked in front, but no one was in them. The door to the warehouse began to open…

Chapter 12

"Stop."

At Calan's abrupt command, M slowed the car.

"Turn in there," Calan said.

M turned into the gas station where he'd stopped to get gas with Sadie the day they'd gone to the embassy. M must have seen what had caught his attention because he pulled to a stop beside an older Mercedes.

"Port authority?" Reed suggested.

Calan got out and looked into the car, seeing Owen's knife and the gun on the passenger side floor. At least now he knew where she'd gone. And that she was safe. For now. He looked around him. There were no windows on this side of the small kiosk. It wouldn't be long before someone noticed the car, if the attendant hadn't already.

He checked the handle on the passenger-side door. It opened. She hadn't locked it. He leaned inside. She'd also left the keys in the ignition. Her thoughtfulness was unnecessary. She'd stolen a car from port authorities. Seeing that they got it back wouldn't stop her from being arrested. Picking up the gun and knife, he checked around him once again to ensure no one saw and then shut the door and returned to the other car.

"Let's go," he said as he climbed in.

M started driving.

"She must have walked to the embassy," Merrick said.

Calan sure hoped she made it and was still there. He bent forward to put the weapons into his duffel bag, which he had stuffed at his feet, and then took out his passport. One of them anyway.

After parking along the street just down from the embassy, M turned to Calan. "Maybe it's better if just you go."

"I wouldn't have it any other way. Give me fifteen."

"Got it."

Leaving the car, Calan jogged to the guarded gate that was open because it was during business hours now. He showed his passport and found his way to security. Once through that, he approached one of two clerks working a reception desk.

He greeted her in English.

She smiled. "Well, hello."

Calan recognized the smile as one only a woman physically attracted to a man would have. "I'm looking for someone. Can you help me?"

"That depends. Are you looking for the woman you came here with before?" the clerk asked.

Calan didn't remember her, but she obviously remembered him. "Yes."

"She was just here. She left. Her passport was ready. I'm sorry you missed her. Did you just want to make sure she received her passport?"

"Where did she go?"

"I don't know. My guess is the airport. The duty officer got her a taxi."

Calan didn't like that at all. What if Dervishi had sent some of his men after the officer and pried him for information? Or threatened him to tell them when Sadie came to pick up her passport? Or had the taxi driver been waiting for one or both of them to go to the embassy?

"Can I talk to him?"

"I'm sorry, he's left for the day."

That couldn't be a good thing. "Thanks."

"Hope you haven't lost her," the woman called after him. "But if you have, I get off at five. It gets lonely in this country."

Without acknowledging her last comment, he turned and left the embassy. Back at the car, he lowered himself inside and M started driving.

"We noticed someone across the street. Might be nothing but it didn't look good," M said.

They had her. Calan rubbed his face. The gravity of it descended on him. An all-too-familiar desperation threatened to grip him. Not again. He couldn't go through this again.

"Looks like it's time to pay Dervishi a visit," Owen said from the backseat.

"She took a taxi from here," Calan said, clinging to the very small hope that it had been legitimate and she was on her way to the airport.

"Could have been one of Dervishi's," M pointed out. As if he needed to.

Calan exchanged a look with him. M was a realist and he didn't think Sadie was on her way to the airport. But what if she was? Calan didn't want to waste precious time being wrong.

"She'll be fine if she makes it to the airport," M said, sounding uncharacteristically reassuring. "We can catch up to her wherever she goes."

And Calan realized how transparent he was being. He cared for her on a level that rivaled past feelings. The thought of her captured by Dervishi crippled him. The thought of never seeing her again made him want to roar.

He should have never left their cabin yesterday morning. He should have known she'd be vulnerable after the way they'd made love. He should have known she'd assume the wrong thing. That he'd want or need to part ways as soon as they reached the States. Maybe if he'd have known what he wanted and needed where she was concerned, he wouldn't have.

But he did now. And he'd be damned if anyone was going to take that from him again.

M was right. If Dervishi didn't have her, then she'd made it onto a plane safely and they could catch up to her.

"All right. Let's take care of Dervishi."

M nodded. "Let's finish this."

Dervishi's sprawling estate made a loud statement about the wealth of the man who resided there. A long driveway curved in a half circle in front of the house. The white stone exterior topped with a red tile roof was contemporary in design, with a grand covered entrance flanked by towering turrets.

M drove the car to a stop where a doorman waited. There was no guard station. That said a lot about his confidence. He wasn't afraid of anyone coming after him. Not many would dare. But there had to be plenty of guards roaming the property.

Calan stood from the car with the others.

"May I help you?" the doorman asked.

"We're here to see Mr. Dervishi," M said.

"Is this business?"

"Yes."

"He isn't expecting anyone."

"Tell him Calan Friese is here to see him," Calan said.

The doorman nodded once and went to the door, where he opened it and spoke to a woman inside. The doorman turned and, saying nothing, simply stood outside the once again closed door. Clever disguise for a guard.

Moments later the door opened and a man appeared, telling the guard in Albanian to let them by.

"This way," he said in accented English to Calan and the rest.

They followed the man into an open, marble-floored entry with a ceiling that rose to the roof. Grand stairs led up on both sides to the second level, an open library visible from below. Three archways on the first floor led to different areas of the home.

The man led them to the stairs on the left, and at the top Calan saw Dervishi standing with two armed men in front of a huge contemporary desk, beyond which a wall of windows offered a view of the mountains in the distance.

Another bit of evidence that he wasn't worried about his safety. The desk faced the room, which meant when he sat there, he had his back to the window. That made the person who sat there an easy target for his enemies. But Dervishi wasn't an easy target.

"Who are you?" Dervishi asked, his eyes passing over each man.

Calan exchanged a glance with M, who moved forward with the plain folder containing all the information they'd gathered on him, including the information on Dharr and his expanding organization, even after his death. The man to Dervishi's left took it from him and then handed it to Dervishi.

"What is this?" Dervishi asked. "Which one of you is Mr. Friese?"

"I am," Calan said. Didn't he already know?

"Am I supposed to recognize your name?" He sounded annoyed. "Why did you come here? Why have I allowed you into my home?"

M met Calan's glance again. Something was wrong.

Reed and Owen each moved in opposite directions on either side of Calan and M. Merrick moved beside M. When Reed and Owen went too far into the room, too close to Dervishi, his men pushed the lapels of their suit jackets aside to reveal their pistols.

Reed and Owen stopped.

"Where is she?" Calan asked Dervishi.

"Who?" He looked down at the file, opening it to read. After a moment, he lifted his head with an angry scowl. "You think you can come into my home and threaten me? Flaunt your men and make demands I know nothing about? I have killed men for lesser offenses."

"All we want is the woman," Calan said.

"What woman?" His perplexed and aggravated tone sounded genuine.

Why would he play games when millions of his money was missing? "Sadie Mancini."

Dervishi's expression remained perplexed. "I do not know of a Sadie Mancini. I do not know any Mancinis. Who is she? And why do you think I would know where she is?"

"One of your men kidnapped her," Merrick replied this time.

"He doesn't know you," M muttered to Calan.

Calan met his gaze in acknowledgment. If Dervishi

didn't know him and Sadie, did he know about the deal Dharr had worked with Zhafa?

"My men, you say?" Dervishi pinned each of the men in the room with a questioning and demanding look. Each one shrugged or shook their head.

"I do not know anyone named Sadie Mancini," the man who'd led them here said.

"Or Calan Friese," said the man to Dervishi's right.

Dervishi stepped closer, taking the file with him, closing it and holding it up like a torch, anger blazing. "Someone should explain this to me."

Calan sensed each of his teammates studying their opponents. This could get ugly fast.

"Gjerji Zhafa arranged a meeting with Abu Dharr al-Majid at an abandoned warehouse in Tirana." He let that sink in a while.

It didn't take long. Dervishi had seen enough of the file to know Dharr was a wanted terrorist in the United States.

"Why did Gjerji arrange a meeting with such a man?"

"I came to Albania because I was tracking Dharr. I followed him to the warehouse and saw him come out with a suitcase after the meeting. I didn't know until after I killed him that the suitcase contained about two and a half million euros."

"Why did you kill this man?"

"My reasons aren't important now. What's important is I find Sadie."

"And you say Gjerji planned to do business with this man? Dharr you call him."

"Yes."

"And you stopped it."

"Yes, but only by chance."

"Where is the suitcase?"

"In a safe place."

Dervishi's brow lowered to an ominous shadow over his eyes. Calan watched as his mind put the pieces together. At last he turned his head. "Kostandin, how is it possible that I know nothing of a two-point-five million euro transaction?"

"I do not know, sir. Gjerji did not tell me anything."

Dervishi turned his question to the other two.

"I did not know either."

"Nor I."

Dervishi faced Calan again. "Where did Gjerji get the money?"

Calan grunted. "You expect me to know? Where did he take Sadie?"

Dervishi's brow retreated to a calmer location on his forehead and a stare-down ensued.

"Kostandin," Dervishi finally said.

"Yes, sir."

"Have someone search Gjerji's home and question anyone who has seen him recently. Ask them to take a look at his finances, too."

"Right away, Mr. Dervishi."

Kostandin left the open library while Dervishi continued to bore into Calan's eyes. "Where is this abandoned warehouse?"

Calan told him the location in Tirana.

"It is not familiar to me."

"Then it appears one of your own has been working independently." Without Dervishi's knowledge. Calan almost cheered. That would work in their favor.

"Yes. It does, does it not? My only question is why?"

"How many reasons are there in an organization like yours?"

Dervishi's mouth curved into a cynical smile. "You have no fear, Mr. Friese. I like that in a man." He glanced back at his men and then faced forward again. "Why don't we all take a ride to this warehouse and see if we can put the question in front of the one who can answer it?"

Calan turned to M, who gave a single nod of his head. Merrick did the same. Owen nodded when Calan met his gaze, and finally Reed.

To Dervishi, Calan said, "Agreed."

Dervishi handed him the folder. "I have no use for this garbage. Perhaps you should give it to Gjerji."

Before the driver came to a stop in front of the warehouse, Sadie opened the back door and jumped. Her foot twisted as she landed. Losing her balance, her hip slammed to the ground and she rolled. She scraped her hands and bumped her knees.

On her behind, she looked toward the warehouse. Four men were running toward her. She scrambled to her feet and made a run for it toward the street. If she could make it to one of the buildings…

"Help!" she yelled.

Two cars drove by, but no one was on the sidewalk.

"Help me!" she yelled louder.

A man emerged from a rundown jewelry store, lighting a cigarette. He looked over at her just as a man from behind grabbed her arm. She tripped and started to fall, but the man hauled her upright, pulling her back against his chest and hooking a meaty arm around her neck.

She gripped his arm and tried to ease the pressure off her throat, letting go to wave at the man across the street. He had to help her. But he just leaned against the side of the building, smoking and watching the scene unfold in the abandoned parking lot of the warehouse.

The driver of the taxi drove to the exit of the parking lot and without a glance back, turned the way he'd come and vanished.

One of the four men strode in front of her, looking across the street. He pushed the sides of his jacket apart with his hands on his hips.

The man across the street took another puff off his cigarette and tossed it to the ground. Pushing off the building, he went back inside.

He wasn't going to help her? Maybe he'd call someone.

When she turned and faced the man in front of her she recognized him. Zhafa. His dark, beady eyes instilled fear with their superior confidence. This time she didn't have Calan to come and rescue her.

"You and I have something to finish," he said. "It was so good of you to make this easy for me."

By leaving Calan and his team, she'd made herself vulnerable to this. But if the duty officer at the embassy hadn't betrayed her, she'd be at the airport by now.

"Take her inside," Zhafa said to the man holding her.

He forced her to walk with him behind the other two.

Sadie fought his grip but he was too strong. What if she managed to get free? Would they shoot her?

Inside the warehouse, she saw that it was for the most part empty. There were a few crates packed with things on one side and a table with four chairs nearby. Two windows along the back were boarded. The other six were dirty, like the cracked concrete floor.

The man holding her forced her to the table and then shoved her onto one of the chairs.

"Have a seat," Zhafa said.

Seeing rope and a pruning shears on the table, Sadie stood and pushed the chair out of her way, backing toward the crates.

"There is nowhere to go," Zhafa said, and then he said to the two other men, "make her sit."

All of them wore suits, like every other time she'd seen Zhafa. The man who'd forced her into the warehouse was the tallest and trimmest. He also had blond hair and blue eyes, which set him apart from his shorter, rounder, darker cohorts. The two who approached her now looked Arabic, with long, stringy beards and black eyes. They looked like brothers, with one older than the other.

It was the younger one who gained ground on her first. She ran around the crates and stopped on the other side when the blond man blocked her way.

The young Arabic man gripped her arm and the blond stepped aside, sweeping his arm with a half bow as if he were a gentleman allowing a lady to go first.

"Pig," she spat.

He grinned and the young man propelled her forward. At the chair, she sat.

"Tie her."

The blond man took her hands and pulled them behind the chair, though she resisted as much as she could. He might as well have been holding doll arms, it was that easy for him to tie her wrists. Sick fear and helplessness almost made her beg to be free.

When he finished and Sadie was left to writhe her hands against the tight restraint, Zhafa bent down.

"There now. Why don't you tell me where my money is?"

"I don't know where it is."

He smiled. "Tell me where it is, or my friend here will

start removing your fingers one at a time. And when you have no fingers left, he will begin to disembowel you."

Sadie held on to her courage. "Then you'll never find your money."

Zhafa straightened. "How did you meet Mr. Friese?"

"I met him at a hotel bar."

He measured her reply for a moment. "Are you sure you aren't working with him?"

"Are you kidding? Of course I don't work with him."

"He is well connected for a man who is no longer with the Army."

"Yes, and if you're smart, you'll let me go and forget about Calan." She had no idea where she was getting this brazenness.

"How did he manage to have a plane waiting for him?"

"Beats the hell out of me."

"And the yacht?"

"How should I know? I'm not his secretary."

He backhanded her so fast she didn't have time to brace herself. She grunted with the impact, tendrils of hair falling over her cheek. She shook her head to get it out of the way.

"Tell me where my money is."

The blond man picked up the pruning shears and twirled it in front of her face.

She looked up at him. "You're going to have to untie me to use that."

"You have an insubordinate mouth for a woman who is about to die a slow and painful death."

Sadie looked toward the door, wishing desperately that Calan would find her. But he wouldn't. He didn't know where she went and he didn't know Zhafa had captured her, much less where she'd been taken.

"All you need to do is tell me where my money is. I will let you go."

Sure he would. He'd let her go. Right after he killed her. She didn't say anything. Seconds ticked onward, closer to her impending murder.

"Untie one of her hands and remove the small finger on her left hand," he said to the blond man, who untied her.

She wrenched her hands, trying futilely to get away. Another man held her left hand while the blond man retied her right. Then he slapped her left hand down on the table.

Sadie screeched and kept her hand in a fist. Her palm was on fire from scraping herself earlier. The blond man pried her pinky finger out and spread it out onto the table.

"No!"

"Where is my money!" Zhafa roared.

"I told you I don't know, and if you hurt me, do you think Calan will tell you?"

"No, you are going to tell me. Now where is it? I am tired of these games." He nodded to the blond man.

Sadie screamed just as a bang echoed in the warehouse.

The blond man released her and straightened. Calan charging through the door he'd just kicked open with a flood of men on his heels was a sight she'd never forget. She frantically brought her hand around the back of the chair and began to work on the knot tying her other hand.

Zhafa raised his weapon and so did his men. But when Dervishi entered the warehouse, walking slow and surrounded by ten or more armed men, he lowered it and dropped it to the concrete floor.

"Calan," she breathed as he came to her.

He knelt and helped her free her hand. She slid off

the chair and onto her knees and then threw herself into his arms.

"Calan."

"Sadie. Don't ever leave me like that again." He kissed her.

Did he mean it? She leaned back and took his face between her hands. "Calan." She said his name instead of something else she'd regret.

She loved him?

She couldn't possibly this soon. It was just the excitement, the tantamount rush of relief that he was here and no one was going to chop off her finger.

"Are you all right?"

She nodded, pressing a kiss to his lips. He slid his hands down her arms and pulled hers from around him. He held her palms up and saw the bloody scrapes there. If he were a dragon, fire would have poured from his nose. His brow shot down and his eyes beamed fury. He shifted his now deadly gaze to Zhafa.

That's when Sadie realized everyone was watching them.

Dervishi's men had Zhafa and his men at gunpoint. Dervishi stood in white slacks and a white jacket over a black shirt, one hand tucked in his pocket, quietly and calmly observing them.

But he soon turned his attention to Zhafa. "It would seem you've made someone upset."

Zhafa said something in Albanian.

"Speak English so my guests can understand you," Dervishi demanded.

Guests? Sadie looked to Calan, but he was still focused on Zhafa, who had hesitated.

"I can explain," Zhafa finally said to Dervishi.

"Explain," Dervishi mocked, walking to stand in front of

him. Two of his men accompanied him, the barrels of their automatic rifles aimed at Zhafa, should he try anything. "Yes, I'd like you to explain what you were planning to do with my money."

A cell phone rang and a man standing behind Dervishi answered.

"It was a harmless business deal," Zhafa said. "I had a chance to make some extra money, that's all."

The man behind Dervishi spoke into his cell phone but was too quiet for Sadie to hear.

"With two-point-five million euros?" Dervishi's eyebrows rose. "A little extra money?"

"I did not steal from you."

"Where did you get it, then?"

"It was mine."

The man who'd taken the call lowered the phone without disconnecting. "Sir."

Dervishi kept his eyes on Zhafa. "Yes?"

"After a little persuasion, his girlfriend told us he was skimming off one of your hotels. The one he managed for you."

"Well, now we know where the money came from."

"I didn't take any money from you. The bitch is lying. I sold my own product to earn that money."

"Using the money you skimmed off my hotel?"

Zhafa remained silent. He was cornered and he knew it.

"She also heard him talking to his friends about taking you down," the man who'd taken the call added. "We have people at his bank right now."

"Good work, Kostandin." Dervishi again turned to Zhafa.

Sadie would have shrunk away from all that power and control.

"What do you suppose the bankers will say?"

Still, Zhafa didn't speak.

"And what about anyone who's worked with you? Helped you deceive me. Do you think they will tell me the truth if I offer to spare their lives?" He looked at the men with Zhafa. The blond man glanced fearfully at Zhafa and back at Dervishi.

"What were you planning to do once you were on your way, making money with your new friends?" Dervishi asked. When Zhafa had no answer, he continued. "Compete with me? Enlist a terrorist to use his body as a bomb? Were you hoping to kill me?"

Zhafa's mouth tightened and his eyes were intense with anger. Was he angry that he'd been caught?

"You think you have what it takes to run my organization?"

"Mr. Dervishi—"

"Answer me!" Dervishi shouted, his voice echoing in the warehouse.

"I would run it so others could profit, not only you."

Sadie fleetingly turned her head into Calan's chest, bracing for what was to come. It was a mistake confessing that to someone like Dervishi.

Calan began to rise, holding her arms and helping her do the same. When they both stood, he slipped his arm around her waist and she stayed close to him, putting one arm around him, too, and curling her hand against his chest so her scrapes didn't rub against the material. When no gunfire sounded, she dared to watch Dervishi and Zhafa go head to head again.

"You don't like working for me? Have I been unfair to you? Treated you so poorly? Not paid you handsomely enough?"

"That is not—"

"You turn to greed and now you've betrayed me."

"I did not betray you."

"No? I do not see it that way."

Sadie noticed the subtle movement of Calan's teammates, positioning themselves apart from each other, dispersing themselves evenly among Dervishi's men.

"Nobody does business behind my back. You work for me. Everything goes through me first."

"My business has nothing to do with yours."

"That is not what I have discovered today, Gjerji. What I have discovered is that you have stolen from me and have desires to overthrow me."

Zhafa put his hands up and looked at each of Dervishi's men. "I did not betray you." He spoke pleadingly in Albanian.

"Kill him."

Zhafa spoke again in Albanian, this time more rapidly and pushing his palms forward, a motion to stop Dervishi from what he was about to do.

Calan pulled Sadie against his chest as several shots went off, a cacophony of sound ricocheting off the high metal walls of the warehouse. She turned to look over her shoulder and saw Zhafa lying on the floor, splatters of blood dotting the concrete. She stifled a cry of horror, uncertain if the man had deserved to be exterminated so ruthlessly, despite what he might have done to her. In her mind she knew it was inevitable, but the humanitarian in her couldn't let go of the hope for good.

"Take the rest of them back to the estate," Dervishi said.

As four of the men herded the blond man and his friends out of the warehouse, Sadie wondered what fate awaited them. Whatever lay in store for them, it probably wouldn't be pleasant.

"And now there's the matter of my money," Dervishi said.

Three of his men moved to stand closer but kept their guns aimed high. Still, the movement triggered a reaction from M and the rest of the team. They turned their weapons on Dervishi and his men, which were now fewer in number since the others had taken Zhafa's men away.

Dervishi held his hand up when his men aimed their weapons, too. "We have no problem here. I am indebted to you for exposing Zhafa and his treachery. But he has taken something that belongs to me."

"I'm afraid we can't give you the money," Calan said.

Dervishi lifted his eyebrows, making his eyes incredulous but not any less threatening.

"It would go against the policy of my employer. I mean no disrespect, but that money was intended to fund terrorism."

"I do not use my money to fund terrorism."

No, but he used it for drug trafficking and Lord only knew what else. Sadie waited to see what Calan would do next.

"Again, I mean no disrespect."

"But you won't return my money."

"I'm sorry. No."

Sadie tensed while Dervishi merely contemplated Calan. Several agonizing seconds drifted by.

"Then perhaps we can work out another solution," Dervishi suggested. "You've done me a great service today. I reward those who serve my interests. Keep the money, and do me one favor."

"There are lines I can't cross."

"I understand. But were there ever to be a situation

where I might need your assistance in some way…nothing unscrupulous, perhaps information. Perhaps an innocent errand. I cannot predict the need. I wish only to have the opportunity to call upon you. As a friend."

Calan smiled. "I would welcome it. But I would also caution you that I may have to decline. There are lines, as I've said."

"Yes, yes. I understand about lines. But I cannot let so much money slip away without some kind of investment in return."

"I will honor any request you have that is in my ability to accommodate."

Dervishi stepped forward and extended his hand. Calan took it and they shook on the agreement.

"In my business, a man's word is as good as his signature."

"In mine, men who cross the wrong lines are my enemy."

The not-so-subtle insult hardened Dervishi's eyes. He was a man who crossed lines. He just hadn't crossed Calan's yet. Calan's boldness may have pushed a little too far.

But Dervishi let the comment go. "We do not have to be friends to help each other. You have exposed Gjerji's treachery to me. Had he been allowed to carry out his plan, he could have done much more damage. He was one of my top men." He looked down at Zhafa's body. "You never know when your friends are going to turn on you." He raised his gaze. "I consider this a worthy cost." Handing Calan one of his business cards, he then extended a pen.

Calan wrote his cell number on it. Then he handed the card back.

Dervishi took it. "Have a safe trip home, Mr. Friese."

Sadie sagged with relief.

"Thank you." Calan guided her around Zhafa's body.

"Clean up this mess," Dervishi bellowed to his men. "I want to be home in time to see my daughter."

M and the others took up the rear after she and Calan passed. Outside, Sadie felt a huge weight lift off her. Nothing was standing in her way of leaving now. She had her passport—her real one—and Calan had no reason to stop her.

But she wished he did. A nonviolent one. Her mood swung low again. When had she ever been that lucky? Never. So why would anything change now? She'd go her way and he'd go his. He'd probably drop her off at the airport now. And she'd never see him again.

Shouldn't that make her happy? She'd risked a lot getting away from him. What was so different now?

Don't ever leave me like that again...

Chapter 13

M parked near the main terminal of Andoni International Airport. On the way here it had been decided that M would pilot them home. Along with his spying abilities, he'd somewhere along the line learned to fly planes. Sadie had told them she'd rather fly commercial, but M had insisted they personally see to it she made it home.

Calan sat next to her in the car. He hadn't said much. He'd barely looked her way, either. His energy radiated the need to be away from her. Now that he knew she'd be safe, nothing buffered the tragedies of his past, the very things that kept his heart locked away from her.

She got out with the rest of them, going to the trunk to get her duffel bag. But Calan took hold of her wrist, careful to avoid her scraped hand, which they'd cleaned up and put ointment on before leaving for the airport. He pulled her back while the others gathered their things. She looked at him, startled.

M slung a bag over his shoulders and smiled at Sadie.

"Nice to meet you," Merrick said, extending his hand and then remembering her hands and hugging her instead.

"Take care of our boy," Owen said. "No more handcuffs." He winked.

George chuckled. "Invite us to the wedding."

"Wh—"

"See you in a couple of weeks," M said to Calan, shaking his hand. "It's been a pleasure working with you. I hope we have the chance again. We make a good team."

"I agree. Thanks for everything."

George gave a nod of farewell. Owen and Merrick started for the terminal. M tossed Calan the car keys and followed.

Watching their retreating backs, Sadie turned to Calan. "What…why…" She pointed to the men. "What's going on, Calan?"

He grinned. "Get in."

"Why? Where are we going?" He was making her go with him again?

"On vacation."

She wasn't sure she liked that. What did he think they'd do? Have a two-week affair and then split up?

"Get in."

What else could she do? She didn't want to try to fly home from this airport. A mobster's airport.

She got in the car.

In Durres, they passed through customs with ease. The yacht they'd commandeered from Zhafa was now docked near the marina building. But Sadie hadn't worried. She was legal again and on her way home. The ferry took the rest of the afternoon to reach Bari, and now she walked with Calan at the marina.

She'd stopped trying to get him to tell her why he was making her go with him. He wasn't going to tell her. She did wish he'd put her out of her misery, though. At least tell her why he was doing this…keeping her with him just like he had before. Only now there was no danger lurking.

At a pretty seventy-five-or-so-foot yacht called *Bellamy*, he stepped onto the swim deck, turning to offer his hand. Sadie didn't have to take it, but she did. He let her go ahead of him up the portside stairs leading to the aft deck, where a blue bench seat lined the stern with two wood-planked chairs and a table before it.

"Is this where M put the money?" she asked as she entered the main salon, with its grand ceiling and plush brown and blue sectional and a pair of chairs. Beyond was a modern galley with white cabinetry and a snack bar with stools. There was also a dining table.

"Yes."

"Aren't you worried how you're going to get it to the United States?"

"It's already there by now."

She sent him a questioning look.

"We had a courier pick it up and ship it to TES."

"That simple, huh?"

"Helps to have the right connections."

She nodded, wandering toward the galley and the wine rack she'd spotted. When she picked out an Italian red, Calan took it from her and opened it for her. She watched his face as he worked. He poured her a glass and then himself one.

When he held his glass, his eyes moved to hers.

Going to one of the snack bar stools, she sat. He sat to her left.

"This brings back memories," he said.

They were on stools, he to her left, just like at the hotel

bar. Eyeing him askance, seeing the sparkle of flirtation in his eyes, she sipped her wine and then lowered the glass.

"When are you going tell me what this is all about?" she asked.

"Do you want to leave?"

She sighed. Yes, she did, but only to protect her heart. No, she didn't because she was too curious and hopeful at the moment.

"I don't want you to leave," Calan said.

Sadie sipped her wine, uncertain.

"What is this, Calan? I've come this far with you. Tell me why I'm sitting on a yacht with you in Italy."

"I thought we'd stop at a few places. Here in Italy. Greece. Spain. After a couple of weeks, we can go home."

"You mean when you're finished with me?" She had to know his intentions. Enough was enough.

"I doubt I'll ever be finished with you."

I don't want you to leave.

"I don't know what the future holds for us, Sadie. All I know is I don't want to stop seeing you and right now I don't think I'll ever want to."

Stronger hope pushed at her defenses. It's what made her stay with him. "Calan, you've lost two women you loved."

"Yes, but that doesn't mean I can't love again. I see that now."

"I don't want to be a transitional phase to you."

"You won't be."

"We've only known each other for a week."

"Then let's make it a month. A year. The rest of our lives."

The rest of our lives…

Oh, to be able to explore that with him, to have a real relationship, with someone who genuinely liked her…

"Even if you leave now, you won't be something transitional to me," he continued. "You mean more to me than that. A lot more. I want to see where it leads." He hesitated. "Do you?"

This was like choosing the people she associated with. Friends. Boyfriends. She hadn't been very good at it before. Why would now be any different? Except Calan was different. Where the people before him hadn't been worth the risk, he was.

"If you want to leave now, I won't stop you. That's why we haven't left Bari yet. I need it to be your decision. It's up to you."

Sipping her wine, she made him wait. She had to be sure. She put her glass down and looked over at him. There was one more thing she had to do before she could put her uncertainty to rest.

"I need to call my dad."

Calan studied her face but went along with her. "All right." He reached for his duffel bag that he'd put on the snack bar and pulled out a satellite phone.

She took it and dialed her dad's cell number.

"Robert Mancini."

"Dad?"

"Sadie?" his voice boomed. "Is that you?"

"Yes."

"Sadie Faye. Are you all right? I'm so sorry about leaving you in Albania. Please tell me you're all right. Where are you now? I'll make any arrangements you need."

"I'm fine, Dad."

"What happened? Why aren't you home yet? When I hadn't heard from you, I was so worried."

"Well..." she looked over at Calan. "Something happened."

Silence stretched over the line. "What is it this time?" There was that impatience again.

"I met someone."

"You always meet someone. What's he done to you?"

"He helped me. I met him the night you turned your back on me. I had to wait for a new passport, and now we're taking a vacation together."

Calan smiled when she said that.

"You just met this man. Are you sure you're safe with him? I don't want to get another call, Sadie."

"You won't. I'll never call you again for help." She wasn't trying to be snide. That was the truth. She didn't need to call him. She never had. It had only been an absurd need for his approval that had kept her so close to him. Being close to her father wasn't the issue, but being close to him on her terms, was. He had to accept her for who she was, artist or not.

Calan had shown her that. She was fine on her own.

"Sadie." She heard his contrition. "I didn't turn my back on you. I know it was wrong to leave you in a country like Albania. You have no idea how I've regretted that. I've been going out of my mind wondering where you were and if you were all right."

"I'm fine. That's why I called. To let you know." And to confirm that it wasn't her choices that were wrong.

"Who is this man you're with? How did you meet him?"

"Calan. He's a…he's a business analyst." She nodded and smiled.

She could tell Calan was enjoying this.

"I'd feel better if you came home now. I'll wire you some money."

"I don't need any money. I have my own."

"Where are you?"

"I'm on a yacht in Italy."

There was a brief silence. "Don't tell me you've met another Adam Krahl."

"No. This one is different."

"That's wonderful to hear, Sadie. All I've ever wanted was for you to be happy. Do you know that?"

"We'll talk more when I get back."

"When will that be?"

She looked up at Calan. "I don't know. I'll call you when I do."

She said her farewell and handed Calan the phone. "Thanks."

"Don't mention it."

Swiveling on the stool, she faced him. "There's something I need to ask you."

"Okay." He waited but she could tell he was on the edge of his seat. He was going to love her question.

"Are you a nice guy?" she asked.

He grinned, recognizing the question she'd asked him in the hotel bar. "That's one way to put it."

She smiled back, that crazy, delicious infatuation burning strong again. "Are you going to ask me to have dinner with you now?"

"How about if I just walk you to our room?"

This was going to be such a good night. "And in the morning, I want to meet you somewhere for breakfast."

"Okay. I'll have our crew set it up on the sundeck."

She shook her head. "You have to call me from the restuarant."

He chuckled again. "I can do that."

Good. She had to hear his voice. She leaned closer to him. "And in case you haven't figured it out yet, we're starting over."

He moved closer, too. "No, we're taking this from

where we left off." He kissed her and her head swooned. Without danger looming, the only thing they needed to concentrate on was each other. And she was going to savor every moment.

"Go tell our captain that we're ready to go."

* * * * *

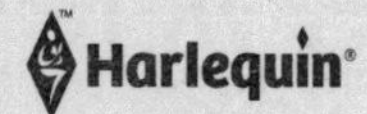

ROMANTIC

SUSPENSE

COMING NEXT MONTH

Available May 31, 2011

#1659 ENEMY WATERS
Justine Davis

#1660 STRANGERS WHEN WE MEET
Code Name: Danger
Merline Lovelace

#1661 DESERT KNIGHTS
***Bodyguard Sheik* by Linda Conrad**
***Sheik's Captive* by Loreth Anne White**

#1662 THE CEO'S SECRET BABY
Karen Whiddon

HRSCNM0511

"THANKS FOR NOT TURNING ON THE LIGHTS," Tyler said. "I'm a mess."

"Not in my book." Even in low light, Alex had a good view of her yellow shirt plastered to her body. It was all he could do not to reach for her, mud and all. But the next move needed to be hers, not his.

She slicked her wet hair back and squeezed some water out of the ends as she glanced upward. "I like the sound of the rain on a tin roof."

"Me, too."

She met his gaze briefly and looked away. "Where's the sink?"

"At the far end, beyond the last stall."

Tyler's running shoes squished as she walked down the aisle between the rows of stalls. She glanced sideways at Alex. "So how much of a cowboy are you these days? Do you ride the range and stuff?"

"I ride." He liked being able to say that. "Why?"

"Just wondered. Last summer, you were still a city boy. You even told me you weren't the cowboy type, but you're…different now."

HBEXP0611

He wasn't sure if that was a good thing or a bad thing. Maybe she preferred city boys to cowboys. "How am I different?"

"Well, you dress differently, and your hair's a little longer. Your face seems a little more chiseled, but maybe that's because of your hair. Also, there's something else, something harder to define, an attitude…"

"Are you saying I have an attitude?"

"Not in a bad way. It's more like a quiet confidence."

He was flattered, but still he had to laugh. "I just admitted a while ago that I have all kinds of doubts about this event tomorrow. That doesn't seem like quiet confidence to me."

"This isn't about your job, it's about…your…" She took a deep breath. "It's about your sex appeal, okay? I have no business talking about it, because it will only make me want to do things I shouldn't do." She started toward the end of the barn. "Now, where's that sink? We need to get cleaned up and go back to the house. Dinner is probably ready, and I—"

He spun her around and pulled her into his arms, mud and all. "Let's do those things." Then he kissed her, knowing that she would kiss him back, knowing that this time he would take that kiss where he wanted it to go. And she would let him.

Follow Tyler and Alex's wild adventures in
SHOULD'VE BEEN A COWBOY
Available June 2011 only from Harlequin® Blaze™
wherever books are sold.

HBEXP0611